"What kind of fantasies?" Daniel's voice was silky, coaxing.

The air between them crackled. How would he react if she grabbed the lapels of his jacket and pulled him in for a kiss?

"Flirting lesson number one," she said lightly. "If a woman admits you've starred in her fantasies, she's probably interested."

His mouth curved in a sensual smile. "Probably?"

"Gaze can be a good indication of desire," she murmured.

"And if she's looking at my lips like she wants to taste them?"

She gave in to impulse and traced his bottom lip with her finger. He shuddered out a breath, warm on her skin.

Her own breathing was unsteady as she slid her hand down his chest. "Go with your instincts."

Dear Reader,

I love "opposites attract" stories. The chemistry between two people with different viewpoints and personalities can be incredible—if they can stop driving each other crazy long enough to explore it.

When Mia Hayes and Daniel Keegan first met in college, he thought she was a confrontational attention-seeker...who also happened to be distractingly gorgeous. And *she* thought *he* was a disapproving know-it-all...who would be unbelievably sexy if he ever figured out how to cut loose.

Years later, when Daniel runs into Mia at his best friend's bachelor party, the attraction between them is stronger than ever. The resulting affair is blazing hot, but is it only a short-term fling? Or can they embrace each other's differences well enough to fit into each other's lives?

I hope Mia and Daniel's story heats up your winter, and I'd love to hear from you! Join me on Twitter, @TanyaMichaels, or at Facebook.com/authortanyamichaels to chat about books, TV, travel, family and sassy house pets.

Happy reading,

Tanya

Tanya Michaels

Tempting the Best Man

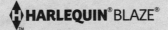
HARLEQUIN® BLAZE®

Recycling programs
for this product may
not exist in your area.

ISBN-13: 978-0-373-79950-3

Tempting the Best Man

Copyright © 2016 by Tanya Michna

Printed in U.S.A.

www.Harlequin.com

Moreno Valley Public Library

Tanya Michaels, a *New York Times* bestselling author and five-time RITA® Award nominee, has been writing love stories since middle-school algebra class—which probably explains her math grades. Her books, praised for their poignancy and humor, have received awards from readers and reviewers alike. Tanya is an active member of Romance Writers of America and a frequent public speaker. She lives outside Atlanta with her very supportive husband, two highly imaginative kids and a bichon frise who thinks she's the center of the universe.

Books by Tanya Michaels

Harlequin Blaze

Good with His Hands
If She Dares
Turning Up the Heat

Harlequin American Romance

Cupid's Bow, Texas

Falling for the Sheriff
Falling for the Rancher
The Christmas Triplets

The Colorado Cades

Her Secret, His Baby
Second Chance Christmas
Her Cowboy Hero

To get the inside scoop on Harlequin Blaze and its talented writers, visit Facebook.com/BlazeAuthors.

All backlist available in ebook format.

Visit the Author Profile page
at Harlequin.com for more titles.

1

"So what's new with you?"

It was the third variation of that question Daniel Keegan had heard in the last fifteen minutes. He'd always dreaded parties where he had to make small talk with strangers, but tonight was proving that catching up with former acquaintances could be just as awkward.

Daniel sipped his beer, stalling. "Um…" Very articulate for a man with a PhD. He could share the story of how he'd proposed a few weeks ago. It had seemed romantic to pop the question at the stroke of midnight on New Year's.

Would've been a lot more romantic if Felicity had said yes. She'd blurted out a panicked no and fled his parents' lavish party.

Or Daniel could discuss how he was being considered for tenure at the university—never mind that he was up against three very qualified candidates all competing for the same vacated spot. Professional triumph would ease the sting of getting dumped, but even with tenure, he'd still be the underachiever in the Keegan family. His older brother was hoping to be the next governor of Georgia.

Fortunately, the opening trombone notes of a classic striptease score interrupted conversation. Men eagerly turned toward the makeshift stage. The chandeliers in the rented ballroom dimmed even further as a spotlight appeared. Leaning against a column toward the back, Daniel tried to look enthusiastic, but part of him would rather be at home in his Buckhead condo, grading papers. *You're the best man. Participation in the bachelor party is mandatory.* Hell, he was just lucky Eli hadn't asked him to plan it.

Tonight's location-hopping party—dinner followed by a private burlesque show before winding down at a jazz club—had been part of a package deal with the same event planning service that was managing Eli's wedding next Saturday. The company had even provided a luxury bus and chauffeur.

A voluptuous redhead in a rhinestone-studded mesh bodysuit sauntered onto the stage, asking where the lucky groom-to-be was and making jokes about the honeymoon. From there, she progressed to audience participation, gathering bits of trivia about Eli's past. The spotlight followed her to the guest of honor, where she sat in Eli's lap and serenaded him with an improvised song about his favorite childhood stuffed animal and the day he got his driver's license. Her lyrics were met with laughter and applause, but the guests really went wild when she introduced the next act—a pair of dancers with large feather fans and teasing smiles.

"Get you another?" A petite blonde waitress, wearing not much more than the women on stage, nodded at the microbrew in Daniel's hand.

"Oh, no thanks." He'd been nursing the same beer since arriving, and it was only half-finished. *Party animal.* "I'm trying to set the record for how long it takes to finish a single drink."

"Designated driver?"

"Nope, just really boring." It was something Sean Clark, head of the university kinesiology department, heckled him about once a week. Sean was the poster child for impulsive fun—which was why Eli hadn't asked *him* to be the best man. Sean was the kind of guy who would lose the rings. Or miss the wedding entirely because he'd skipped town with a hot bridesmaid.

"I'm sure that's not true," the waitress protested. She gave him a slow once-over and a mischievous smile. "You look like you would be very exciting under the right circumstances."

"Maybe you're right," he agreed politely. "Maybe I'll surprise myself." *Liar.* It had been drilled into him from birth that he had a family name and image to protect; he'd repressed his wild side for so long it probably didn't exist anymore.

Another lie. Daniel knew damn well he had a rebellious streak buried deep down. But after so many years censoring himself, if he ever gave in to it, how would he regain his self-control?

"I'll be sure to check back with you later," the waitress promised. "I like surprises."

As she moved on toward the tables clustered in

front, Eli Wallace appeared, clapping Daniel on the shoulder. "Did I see you flirting with the cute waitress?" His approving smile gleamed white against his dark skin. "Progress!"

"Just a bit of friendly conversation."

"At least I can trust you not to get *too* friendly." Eli's smile vanished. "My dumb-ass cousin Terrence got a little handsy with the bartender. I questioned whether to even invite him tonight, but since both of his brothers were coming... Help me keep an eye on him? If he gets too obnoxious, we pour him into a cab and send his ass home."

"Remind me, which one's Terrence?" Daniel and Eli had gone to high school together before ending up as professors at the same university years later; Daniel had met many of the man's relatives in passing, but only knew Eli's parents well.

Eli pointed across the room to a man in a disheveled suit whistling at the dancers from his seat.

"I'll keep an eye out," Daniel promised.

"Thanks, man. If you'll excuse me, I should mingle—and keep some distance between me and the performers. If anyone else ends up in my lap, Bex will kick my ass."

Rebekah was tiny compared to Eli's six-foot-five but the surgical resident was fierce. "Yeah, probably best not to piss off a woman with regular access to scalpels and bone cutters."

Eli laughed, but his amusement gave way to sincerity. "All I want to do is make her happy."

"You will. You guys are great together." Daniel almost winced at the unintentional irony; Eli had said the same to him when Daniel was psyching himself up to propose to Felicity.

Sympathy flashed in Eli's gaze, and Daniel waved his friend away. "Go. You've got other guests to talk to."

Making good on his agreement to watch Terrence, Daniel glanced in the man's direction a few minutes later, but his gaze snagged on the second waitress working the room. She had her back to him, her black hair swishing across her bare shoulders in a straight, shiny fall that reminded him of someone he hadn't thought of in almost a decade. *Mia Hayes.* In college, she'd had hair like that, but streaked with turquoise.

Trying not to ogle, he resisted the urge to compare the waitress's body to Mia's. Déjà vu aside, they couldn't be the same woman. Mia had been in the MBA program. With her intelligence and aggressive nature, she'd probably taken over a company by now. Or a small country. Seeing people from his past tonight had simply triggered a sense of nostalgia.

Still, details about Mia came rushing back with startling clarity. The flaming feather tattoo on the back of her neck, her lush curves, her husky laugh. Her utter disdain for him. Daniel had made a woefully bad first impression, and she'd been unforgiving. The few times they'd been forced to work together in class had only made the situation worse.

Putting aside the past, he checked again on Eli's cousin, who was now stumbling toward the men's room. Free to watch the show, Daniel turned to the stage. A tall woman was asking for volunteers. She and another performer with great comic timing did a parody of a magic act, full of tricks that "failed" and innuendo-laden explanations.

It wasn't long before his undisciplined gaze scanned the crowd for the dark-haired waitress bustling between thirsty guests and the bar. He still hadn't caught a clear look at her face, but her curves were evident even in the dim lighting. Black shorts cupped a generous ass, and although she was probably only average height, the seamed fishnet stockings she wore with sparkly stilettos made her legs appear endless. Anxious to see the purple brocade corset she wore from the front, he considered walking to the bar just to cross her path.

Don't be sleazy. Let the woman do her job.

But then he saw Terrence approach her on unsteady feet. Daniel bolted toward them as Eli's cousin gripped her elbow. Everyone else's attention was on the stage. As Daniel got closer, he heard the man remark in slurred speech on how cold she must be in her outfit and offer a vulgar suggestion of how he could keep her warm.

"If my choices were you or frostbite," the woman said in a low, don't-fuck-with-me tone, "I'd happily freeze to death. Now let go of me before I knee you so hard your dentist will be giving you your next prostate exam."

Daniel was struck by shock and recognition. *"Mia?"*

2

No way. That deep, rich voice slid up Mia's spine like a caress and she whirled around, temporarily forgetting the dipshit she'd been about to neuter. Finding herself eye to V with the unbuttoned collar of a black suit shirt, she lifted her gaze to a chiseled face that had only grown more arresting in the last decade. Her breath caught. "Ta— Daniel?" She'd almost called him Tall, Dark and Disapproving, her private nickname for him in college.

"Glad you remember." He gave her an uncharacteristically warm smile before his expression hardened as he glanced past her to the guy who'd finally released her arm. "You are taking a cab home. Immediately."

"What the hell business is it of yours?" The man thrust out his chin belligerently. "I don't even know you. And—"

Daniel took a step forward, his silvery eyes glittering with menace. "Would you like to step outside where we can get to know each other better?"

Mia was impressed despite herself. Damn, he'd grown up well. Not that they'd been kids when they'd had Psych together. She'd been twenty, and he'd inspired a few *very* adult fantasies. Swallowing hard, she stepped away from both men to regain her composure.

Daniel gave her an assessing look, his gaze sliding over her in a way that made her shiver. Then he turned and led the dipshit away, either to hail him a cab or to pummel him in the parking lot. Either option was okay with Mia. She could take care of herself, but the more she thought about what had happened, the angrier she got. If one of the waitresses who routinely worked for her hadn't called in sick at the last minute, the younger woman would be here now, harassed by unwanted attentions. There was a risk that Mia's hostile words to a guest could get back to the client and upset him—although Mia had more faith in Eli than that—but as a self-employed party planner, Mia could take that risk without fearing reprisals from a boss. Would the waitress have felt free to stand up for herself, or would she have tolerated the pawing because she needed the job? Mia's anger surged higher.

When she saw Daniel return, she abandoned the empty bottles she'd been collecting and strode toward him. "Did you beat him up?" *Wishful thinking.* Rigid rule-follower Daniel Keegan in a fight? Never. Yet he'd looked so deliciously sinister when he'd challenged the guy.

"Of course not. I got him a taxi. Although…" He pursed his lips, unexpected mischief lighting his eyes.

"While I was helping him into the car, he *may* have hit his head. Twice."

She grinned up at him, and when he returned the smile, her pulse fluttered. The pull of attraction was even stronger now than when he'd given a presentation on social motivation and she'd spent the class wondering what it would take to motivate him to misbehave. She'd concluded he wasn't capable of it. Yet here he was enjoying an evening of strippers and booze. *Promising.*

Had he changed over time, or was he only in attendance because he was a friend or colleague of the groom-to-be? Another thought struck her. Was Daniel married? Her gaze slipped to his left hand, and she felt something ridiculously similar to relief when she didn't spot a ring there. Daniel Keegan hadn't been in her life in years—and, even when he had, his role had mainly been judgy classmate—so who cared if he was single?

When she realized the silence between them had become officially awkward, she blurted, "I can't believe I ran into you here."

"Same. I'm surprised you ended up a cocktail waitress. Although, I suppose you—"

Her hackles rose; he'd always been too quick to judge based on superficial appearance, too arrogant in thinking he knew a damn thing about her. "You suppose *what*?"

"Well." He shifted uncomfortably. "Even with your grades, the idea of you in the business world…"

Was what, laughable? Ridiculous? He didn't think she could cut it. Given the *hours* she put in, sacrificing the last few years of a social life to make her party-planning business successful, his offhand dismissal was infuriating.

"Same old Keegan," she snapped. "Still leaping to the nearest conclusion based on cursory observation. What a shame. For half a second, I was thinking about how much fun we could have had if you'd changed."

What kind of fun? The unspoken question kept Daniel rooted to the spot even as Mia spun on her heel and abandoned him to deliver another round of drinks.

Mia Hayes had always been sexy, but tonight— in that outfit, with those glinting amber eyes that alternately threatened and promised—she was lethally seductive. When she'd smiled up at him after he'd admitted Terrence had bumped his head, Daniel had been struck with sheer lust. He'd rarely been on the receiving end of her smiles; he might be willing to bust a few more skulls to see it again.

Unfortunately, based on that final glare, the head she wanted to see bashed was his own. He hadn't meant to insinuate she couldn't be more than a waitress... or that there was anything wrong with waitressing, for that matter. But he'd obviously put his foot in his mouth.

Not the first time.

When she'd knocked on his door in college, looking for his roommate, Daniel had made some assumptions based on the women his roommate usually dated. During small talk while they'd waited, Mia had made a comment about majoring in business and, taking in her blue-streaked hair and controversial fashion choices, he'd legitimately thought she was kidding. Laughing had not endeared him to her.

Twice before the dancers' finale, he tried to approach Mia to apologize, but she evaded him, moving with impressive speed in her high heels. He didn't want to make a scene by cornering her, but as he and the other men boarded the party bus for their next location, he regretted not having the chance to say he was sorry.

"Saw you escort Terrence from the building," Eli said quietly. "Thanks."

Daniel nodded. "Your cousin was having trouble taking no for an answer, and the waitress was about to eviscerate him. Damnedest thing—I went to school with her. Mia Hayes."

"Isn't she great? Not only has she made the entire wedding process painless, she stepped in tonight when one of her servers canceled last minute."

Daniel blinked. "What do you mean 'wedding process'?"

"She's our event coordinator. She arranged everything for tonight and hosted a bachelorette scavenger hunt for Bex." He reached into his wallet and pulled out a business card, which he handed to Daniel.

As Eli continued happily chatting about the arrangements Mia had overseen for next weekend, Daniel stared at the writing on the card. She ran her own company. *So...not a cocktail waitress, then.* Although it had seemed like a valid assumption under the circumstances, he was embarrassed by his reaction to seeing her. When would he learn that Mia Hayes didn't meet simple expectations? On the plus side, he now had the phone number for her office.

Considering their history, further contact could be disastrous. Yet Daniel caught his own grin reflected in the window. He couldn't say whether or not a conversation with her would end in disaster. But he was damn sure it wouldn't be boring.

"How did I let Penelope Wainwright talk me into organizing a formal tea?" Mia asked, grateful to be back in the office before Monday was completely over. After showing her client three potential venues in the Roswell historic district, Mia had lost an hour plodding behind school buses and swearing at afternoon traffic. "High-society crap isn't my area."

Shannon Diaz, receptionist and one-woman IT department, closed a drawer in the metal filing cabinet. "You agreed because she caught you after a weekend of binging on *Downton Abbey* episodes," the brunette reminded her. "And because Penelope is one of our best paying clients. And the tea is a fund-raising event for a good cause. Not to mention, you secretly adore her."

"Ha! Well, I admire a couple of her qualities," Mia relented. The sixty-year-old woman did not suffer fools, for instance. "But she's a pain in the ass to work for— demanding, opinionated…"

Shannon shot her a pointed look over the top of her playfully retro multicolored horn-rimmed glasses.

Mia scowled. "Is it wise to imply *I'm* an opinionated pain in the ass when your job security is in my hands?"

"You'd be lost without me. My job security is just fine."

"Too true." Pausing at Shannon's desk before heading into her office, Mia added, "You know, as wonderful as your *professional* confidence is, don't you think that—"

"Want to hear your messages? No point in wasting office time on my personal life."

"You're brilliant and beautiful and not without a sense of humor. Plus, we already know she likes you. All you have to do is ask her out."

"When I'm ready," Shannon mumbled.

Timing had been a major hurdle between Shannon and Paige. The woman who ran the French café on the third floor of the office building once asked Shannon on a date, but, emotionally raw from recent heartbreak, Shannon had refused more abruptly than intended. By the time she changed her mind a few weeks later, Paige was seeing someone.

"You're both single now," Mia said.

"I'm aware. But what if it's too soon after her breakup? Besides, it's been ages since she asked me out. Who knows if she's even still interested?"

"You—"

"So *about these messages.*" Shannon waved squares of pink paper at her. "A prospective client set up a meeting to get price quotes, Wren had a brainstorm about the venue for her sister's engagement party and Dara Abrams returned your call about flower deliveries." Mia was trying to set it up so that, rather than being thrown out afterward, any remaining live flowers from events she coordinated could be donated to nursing homes. "And a man called after lunch."

Mia arched an eyebrow at the vagueness. Shannon was usually a stickler for details. "Did the man have a name?"

"One assumes. But he didn't leave it."

Even though it was an illogical leap, Mia's mind immediately went to Daniel Keegan. It had been a shock to run into him for the first time since college. There were millions of people in the Atlanta metropolitan area; she and Daniel didn't exactly run in the same circles. He'd looked so damn good. That part wasn't unexpected—his physical appeal had always made her lady parts twitch with interest—but she'd been startled to find that he was even more attractive than she'd remembered. For a few brief, titillating moments, she'd believed the attraction was mutual.

But even if he thought she looked drop-dead sexy in a corset—which, frankly, she did—it was difficult to imagine him contacting her. In the past, he'd wanted as little to do with her as possible.

His loss. She banished all thoughts of Daniel and his mesmerizing eyes and the corded forearms that made her yearn for a look at the muscles hidden beneath his well-tailored clothes. She didn't need mental images of him for fantasy fodder. She had cable.

Mia took the messages. "So what did the mystery caller say?"

"He asked to speak with you and seemed disappointed to hear you were out of the office. In lieu of leaving a message with me or on your voice mail, he asked if I knew when you'd be back. Maybe he's planning to call again. Maybe you have a secret admirer!"

"I've never found the idea of a secret admirer romantic. It actually runs the risk of being a little stalker-y, if you think about it. Someone lurking on the edges of my life but without the nerve to walk up and say hi directly? I'm attracted to people who put their cards on the table." She paused a beat. "Maybe Paige appreciates the direct approach, too."

Shannon sighed. "I'm not ready. And you may sign my paychecks, but you are not the boss of my love life."

"Sorry. You're right." Mia hadn't meant to push so hard, she just wanted to see her friend happy. "I won't bring it up again, I promise. But one last general piece of advice? To get what you want, sometimes you have to step out of your comfort zone."

"I couldn't agree more," said a masculine voice from behind them.

Daniel. Mia spun around, stunned to find him entering the office. Her mouth dropped open, but she couldn't think of anything to say other than *what the hell are you doing here?* which was hardly a polite, professional greeting. She swallowed. "What the hell are you doing here?"

"Stepping out of my comfort zone." He flashed a self-deprecating grin. "I thought maybe I could buy you dinner, if you're not busy after work."

Tempting. Dressed casually in well-worn jeans and a black sweater, he looked every bit as good as he had Friday night. *Where's your pride?* The man had insinuated that she couldn't hold a grown-up job. If she were a petty person intent on making a point, she'd name-drop wealthy Penelope Wainwright. But she didn't care about Daniel's opinion, she just wanted him to go away and take his assumptions with him.

"Actually, tonight I…" She sighed. Fibbing wasn't in her nature. Besides, Shannon was watching with acute interest. After all of Mia's encouragement to take some risks, wouldn't dodging Daniel be hypocritical? "Dinner sounds—" *confusing* "—nice. But I have at least another hour's worth of work to do here."

"No problem." He held up a briefcase. "I noticed on the building directory that there's a café upstairs. I can grab a cup of coffee and get some work of my own done." He wrote down his number so she could text him when she was ready. Then he was gone, leaving her bemused over the turn of events.

"Well." Shannon leaned back in her chair, grinning. "At least one of us has a date."

"I wouldn't call it a date, at least not in the romantic sense. Just two former classmates catching up. Daniel and I went to college together."

"And you never…?" Shannon waggled her eyebrows. "I mean, he's not my type, but *damn*."

Mia resisted the urge to fan herself. Damn, indeed. "Get your mind out of the gutter, Diaz." *There's not room for both of us.* Even back in college, when Mia had told herself she couldn't like anyone as closed-minded as Daniel Keegan, she'd had more than her share of dirty thoughts about the man. Seeing him again stirred up each and every one of them.

Trying to look unfazed, she headed into her office.

But she couldn't focus on work. She didn't know which was more difficult—wrapping her head around Daniel's out-of-the-blue invitation to dinner or trying not to fantasize about dessert.

3

EVEN THOUGH THEY'D agreed Mia would text him, Daniel was still somewhat surprised when her message popped up on his phone. She hadn't looked thrilled to see him when he'd appeared in her office earlier. On some level, he'd expected her to find a reason to cancel. Then again, Mia had never been the sort to make excuses. She meant what she said and said what she meant.

A decade ago, he'd found her bluntness abrasive. But after Felicity blindsided him, dumping him when he'd never realized she had reservations about their relationship, he had a greater appreciation for outspoken females. Mia might be opinionated, but a man would know where he stood with her.

Eager for her company, he hurriedly stuffed graded papers into his briefcase. Instead of waiting for the elevator, he took the stairs and met her in the lobby. She stood against the wall, studying her phone. Between her trench coat and the leather boots that went up almost to the hem of her skirt, she wasn't showing any skin. But the way she carried herself made her as sexy as she had been in fishnet tights and a corset.

When she glanced up, her hazel eyes meeting his, awareness jolted through him. At that moment, asking her out felt like the best decision he'd made in months. "Thanks for agreeing to dinner," he told her. "I hope my showing up in person didn't make you feel obligated to say yes."

Her eyes sparkled with amusement. "No worries on that score. My parents have tried to control me through a sense of obligation for years, with no success."

He felt a stab of envy—would that he could shrug off his own family obligations so easily. "Glad to hear it." Did that mean she *wanted* to go out with him?

She nodded toward his briefcase. "Get a lot of work done?"

No. He'd been too distracted by the prospect of going out with her. "Some."

"What kind of career did you end up with, anyway?"

"I teach."

Lips quirked in a half smile, she studied him in a leisurely perusal that made his skin prickle with heat. He reached for the door, welcoming the January chill.

"You're a professor," she said, as they stepped outside.

"Good guess."

"Well, I can't picture you surrounded by small children. And college is so much more serious than high school."

For a minute, he really wished that he taught teenagers so he could show her he wasn't as predictable as she imagined. *But you are.* Depressing.

On the other hand, coming to see her this evening had been completely out of character. Who knew what other surprises might be in store? "And you're an event planner," he said, curious about the path she'd taken.

She turned to face him, walking backward down the sidewalk. "What would you have guessed? I mean, if we hadn't run into each other and I happened to cross your mind for some reason, what would you have imagined me doing for a living?"

Daniel felt as if the question was a test. He had a history of unintentionally insulting her, which he didn't want to do now, but she wasn't the type of person who would appreciate a disingenuous answer, either. "No idea. But I could have pictured you as a lawyer. You always enjoyed arguing."

Her laugh suggested she was not offended by this assessment. Instead, she winked at him. "I enjoy lots of things, Danny."

His pulse pounded in his ears. He was suddenly very grateful Felicity hadn't accepted his proposal. The fact that Mia's mischievous smile seemed sexier than anything that had happened to him in the past six months proved there had definitely been something missing in his last relationship.

"Why did you come here today?" she blurted. "If it's just because you feel like you owe me an apology for putting your foot in your mouth the other night, don't worry about it. I was already cranky from that jackass trying to—"

"I'm here for fun."

She raised an eyebrow, looking skeptical. He didn't blame her. When was the last time he'd done anything for the sheer hell of it—because it made him smile, because he liked the exhilaration of not knowing what would happen next?

He held her gaze, feeling freer, lighter, than he had in a long time. "You said that if I had changed, we could have had fun together. Maybe I need a change." He'd carefully planned his life, set short- and long-term goals and worked studiously toward them, yet where had his efforts landed him? Single, with a family that would drive him ever crazier as the fall election approached. And as much as he hoped the university's board of regents granted him tenure, stressing about their answer wouldn't improve his chances.

"Daniel Keegan having fun." Mia's tone was light and teasing. "There's a mind-blowing concept." They'd run out of sidewalk, and she paused at the edge of the parking lot. "So where to? Did you have a specific place in mind?"

No. He was officially making this up as he went along. The only place he wanted to be was alone with her, but that seemed like an odd thing to say to a woman he hadn't seen in nearly a decade. "What are you in the mood for?"

"Ever had a plantain s'more?"

"A what, now?"

"Baked plantain, rolled in chocolate, marshmallow and graham cracker crumbs. There's a restaurant about fifteen minutes away that does Latin American and

Caribbean food. They shouldn't be too crowded on a Monday. Excellent dessert menu."

Her priorities amused him. "You always decide where to have dinner based on the desserts?"

"Yes." Her husky tone was both challenge and invitation. "What's wrong with enjoying the evening more because you know it's leading up to something deliciously decadent?"

"I can't argue with that." The longer his gaze held hers, the more he wanted to hear about her ideas of decadence. He broke the connection, glancing toward his car. "I'm, ah, parked over there. Do you want me to follow you to the restaurant?"

"To be perfectly honest, I spent the afternoon in traffic and am in no hurry to get back behind the wheel. Do you mind driving? I can give you directions to the restaurant, then you can bring me back here. If that's not taking you too far out of your way."

"Not at all." He might be out a little later than expected, but that might be a good thing. If he went to bed later than usual, would he stop waking up at three thirty or four in the morning, unable to fall back asleep?

He'd had insomnia since New Year's. During that window of time when he tossed and turned, pretending he might actually fall back asleep, it wasn't Felicity who haunted him so much as his family's faces when he'd told them. *Poor Daniel* had hung in the air like suffocating smog. His two older brothers were both married and unquestionably successful. Had he imagined the hint of smugness in their condolences? Daniel's birthday was in a few weeks, which meant the usual family dinner. God willing, he'd have tenure by then. He would not be the failure in the Keegan family.

He led Mia to his car and opened the passenger door for her, which earned him a bemused smile.

"The polished manners of gallant Daniel Keegan," she said softly.

"Is that a roundabout way of saying I'm old-fashioned?" His own friends called him stuffy. To a free spirit like Mia, he must seem downright rigid.

"It's a roundabout way of saying I'm surprised you're voluntarily spending time with me. I'm not known for demure refinement...as you pointed out more than once when we went to school together."

He flinched. In retrospect, he'd been a bit of a self-righteous ass when he was younger. Luckily, the longer he'd been out of his parents' house, the less he judged others through the Keegans' narrow worldview. When he'd met Mia, he'd found her both fascinating and discomfiting. He'd been raised not to steal attention from his brothers, who were clearly Going Places, raised never to do anything controversial or scandalous. His job was to blend, to be polite and unobtrusively charming.

Mia Hayes did not blend.

When he climbed in on his side of the car, he told her, "I'm sorry if there were times I was a sanctimonious jerk."

"If?" But she smiled, looking pleased by his apology.

"You were so different from most of the girls I'd known." And not because he'd rarely seen tattoos and turquoise-streaked hair at his parents' country club. "You seemed to thrive on friction."

"Under the right circumstances, friction can feel pretty damn good."

His brain lit up with images of bodies rubbing against each other, and it was on the tip of his tongue to say to hell with the restaurant and ask her back to his apartment.

But then she instructed, "Make a left at the intersection," and he shifted his focus to driving. More or less.

As they waited at the red light, he told her, "I know we were never friends in college, but I did admire you. I respected your smarts—"

"Even when I got a higher grade than you did?" she needled.

The gallant response would be *yes*. "On two projects, Hayes." He'd busted his ass to earn an impressive GPA. "As I recall, I finished with a higher final score in both classes we had together."

"Because you were teacher's pet, dutifully regurgitating what the professors told us instead of exploring more divisive interpretations."

"Arguing a premise out of sheer reflex is habit, not proof of intellectual superiority."

"And I suppose when you grade essays and exams, you reward students who mindlessly parrot what you've told them?"

"Of course," he snapped. "For I am an academic god with no patience for mere mortals who think for themselves."

She laughed aloud at his sarcasm. "Good thing we're mature now and finally get along, huh?"

He couldn't believe that she'd provoked him so easily, yet sparring with her was perversely refreshing. "I was *trying* to pay you a compliment."

"Next time, I'll handle the flattery with more grace."

"*Pfft*. What makes you think there will be a next time?"

"Run out of nice things to say about me already, Professor?"

You're audacious and funny and so fucking sexy I can barely keep my eyes on the road. "I don't think 'nice' applies to you."

"You'd be surprised." Her grin was wicked. "I can be very nice when I want to be."

When she smiled like that, there wasn't enough air in the car. His chest constricted. His body tightened with lust, and he gripped the steering wheel harder to keep from reaching for her. If he could've found his voice in that moment, he would have asked what it took to coax her to be nice.

But he was starting to think maybe nice wasn't what he wanted.

DINNER WITH DANIEL was a revelation. Mia couldn't remember the last time she'd had so much fun on a date. *Is this a date?* she asked herself as the waitress set dessert on the table. Daniel's explanation for asking her out hadn't been a burning desire for her company, simply that he needed "a change."

Still, his impersonal reasoning aside, their evening

had the hallmarks of a date. Since Daniel had never been to the restaurant before, they'd decided to sample tapas plates instead of ordering entrées, sliding close together in the curved booth to share food. While enjoying yucca fries, miniature empanadas and grilled beef served with flavorful *chimichurri*, they'd had a lively conversation, discussing literature-based movies and arguing about which format was more successful for each story. Most date-like of all, there was palpable chemistry between her and her smoking-hot companion.

Daniel might spend a lot of his time teaching classes and publishing academic papers, but it was clear from his muscular build and lithe grace that he didn't overlook physical recreation. He'd mentioned weekly basketball games with Eli and jogging the paths around the Chattahoochee River in warmer weather. It was difficult to decide which was sexier—his toned, masculine body or the gleam in his silvery eyes when he teased her. She was discovering he had a much better sense of humor than she would've anticipated. Daniel Keegan in a playful mood was nearly irresistible.

Mia tried not to get bogged down by regrets, but for the first time she wondered what their earlier relationship would have been like if she hadn't had a chip on her shoulder when they'd met. She'd gone off to college angry with her father and her stepmother, wounded at their lack of support when she'd needed it most and betrayed by their attempts to remake her in the image of her oh-so-proper stepsister. *Never gonna happen.*

"Hey." Daniel lightly poked her shoulder. "Did I lose

you somewhere? I could understand if I'd been droning on about Renaissance literature, but I was sharing a quality childhood anecdote from my limited supply. I can count on one hand the number of times my brothers and I indulged in humorous shenanigans."

"Then we have that in common."

"Really? I would have thought your youth was full of shenanigans."

Far fewer than he imagined, and none with her stepsister. "Patience and I didn't have a whimsical relationship."

"Patience being your sister?" He reached for a chocolate-coated slice of plantain.

"Step. It was just me and Dad for years. He remarried the summer before I started high school, and, boom, suddenly I had an older sibling. We're only a year apart in age, but Patience…" Mia couldn't think of a way to describe her that didn't sound petulant.

"Is she bossy? I have lifelong experience being the youngest sibling."

"Patience is shy and soft-spoken. She wouldn't be able to boss around the world's most accommodating personal assistant, much less *me*. We couldn't be less alike." Much to their parents' dismay.

Even now, years after the fact, the memory of her father's words were a raw wound. *I'm not saying that it was your fault, but I can't imagine the same thing would have happened if Patience had been in your situation.*

"I don't want to talk about my family," she said abruptly.

Daniel nodded, unfazed by her harsh tone. Perhaps he'd heard it often enough in college to be used to it. "How did you decide you wanted to be an event planner?"

"By accident. I was interning for a horrible woman who used to pawn off her personal errands on me, everything from picking up her dry cleaning to emptying her cat's litter box—which I firmly refused to do. But then she put me in charge of her parents' anniversary party, and it was more fun than work. I mean, who doesn't love a party?"

He gave her a sheepish look, silently admitting parties weren't his favorite place to be.

But Mia had never been one to back down from a challenge. "I bet I could plan you the perfect party." A successful event meant different things to different guests. One person's backyard kegger was another person's museum wine-tasting. She'd coordinated myriad events, everything from painting parties to bar mitzvahs to themed scavenger hunts.

"My birthday's in early February," he told her, sliding the dessert plate toward her so she could take the last piece. "It's tempting to hire you to plan a celebration instead of going to my parents'. Breaking tradition would probably get me disowned, but…" He hitched a shoulder in a half shrug, suggesting family exile might not be the end of the world.

"My mom hosted my favorite birthday party of all time." It was one of the few vivid memories she had of her mother. "It was for our dog, Sasha."

He grinned. "You had birthday parties for the dog?"

"Not every year. Just that once. It had been a hot-as-hell summer, and I was antsy to start kindergarten." She knew those details more from hearing her dad repeat the story than from her own recollections. "To help me pass the time—and probably for her own entertainment, since I had to be driving her crazy—Mom said we should have a party for the dog. She told me Sasha was turning one, but I have no idea if the dog's birthday was even in July. Mom invited other puppies from around the neighborhood. She organized games and baked a cake for me and my friends in the shape of a giant bone. I still have the picture she snapped in the ten seconds when all the dogs were actually wearing their party hats." Less than six months later, her mother had been killed in a car accident.

Daniel was smiling at her story. "Maybe, subconsciously, you decided then that you wanted to be a party planner."

She tried unsuccessfully to smile back. Her face felt stiff, and her throat was tight. She was glad when the waitress interrupted, bringing their check. Mia offered to pay half, but Daniel insisted that since dinner had been his idea, he should pay.

"Besides," he added, grabbing a couple of mints as they exited, "I owe you. This place is fantastic, and without you, I never would have known it existed."

The restaurant was small and family-owned, on a lot so tiny that parking was several blocks away. "It's true they don't do much advertising." Mia was constantly telling people about the hidden gem, doing her part to keep the place in business. "I'm not even sure they have a website. Thank goodness for repeat customers and word-of-mouth recommendations."

"Word-of-mouth and networking must be important for your business, too. Eli said Bex met you at some friend-of-a-friend event?"

"She was actually a guest at two completely unrelated functions I handled—a baby shower for one of her former sorority sisters and a bachelor auction benefiting the hospital. We hit it off, and she asked me to do their wedding, even though it's not my area of expertise. Theirs will bring me up to half a dozen."

"Seems to me that opportunities for expansion are a sign of a successful company. I'm impressed you've managed to thrive in a customer-based field."

Mia stopped dead on the sidewalk, narrowing her eyes. "Your surprised tone is ever so flattering." Was the man always going to underestimate her?

"Sorry. There was meant to be a compliment in that."

"Must have missed it," she said.

"It's impossible to make everyone happy, right?" He unlocked his car with the key remote as they approached. "I've had more than one student drop my class or complain to the department chair about a grade—although so far, he's upheld all my decisions. In order for you to build clientele, there's a certain amount of people-pleasing inherent in your job. But there must be times you'd rather verbally skewer someone." He opened her door for her, his expression darkening. "Like with that jerk who grabbed you at Eli's party."

He was far from the first. She sighed. "Since he'll also be a wedding guest, I suppose I could have tried to handle that with more diplomacy, but— No, screw that. He didn't deserve tact. Getting groped in college by idiot fraternity guys who considered it flirting was bad enough. But he was a grown-ass man who should know better. Hopefully, he'll think twice next time before making a move on some poor bartender or waitress." *Or babysitter.* Mia clenched her hands, her fingernails digging into her palms as Daniel crossed to the driver's side.

He turned the key in the ignition, his posture tense. "You got groped a lot in college?" Maybe she wasn't the only one with anger issues; from his tone, he sounded like he wanted to go back in time and dole out some fist-based justice.

"Probably less than the average female university student." She'd gained a reputation after pepper-spraying a guy who had trouble processing *no.* "I like sex."

The car jerked unsteadily as they backed out of the parking spot.

"But that doesn't mean I'm willing to have it with just anyone," she continued. "Nor am I required to defend my decision not to have it. I told Shannon earlier today that I respect men who are direct, who aren't afraid to make their attraction known. I've never been mad at a man for showing interest. But when the interest isn't mutual, it's time to back the hell off. Too many guys willfully lie to themselves about what constitutes encouragement. A woman inhaling and exhaling is *not* a sign of burning lust." And a teenager wearing a tank top and shorts on a humid, hundred-degree day was not a sign that she wanted to be pawed at by a man twice her age.

Daniel was quiet as he turned onto the street leading back to her office, and Mia realized she'd been ranting. She hadn't meant to sound so hostile; Daniel hadn't done anything wrong. *He's one of the good ones*. She was pretty sure she'd had the situation at the bachelor party under control, but she appreciated his coming to her aid. Chivalry might be on the endangered species list, but it wasn't extinct.

"So, what should a guy look for as real signs of interest?" he asked, changing lanes.

She eyed him, trying to decide if he was making light of her tirade.

"I just got out of a long-term relationship with a woman I'd been seeing on-and-off since middle school," he told her.

"You're kidding."

"Nope. Our families convinced us to go to the eighth-grade formal together."

Ugh. Mia couldn't imagine dating anyone hand-picked by her parents. No doubt they would have tried to find someone who would be a "good influence" on her.

"My flirting skills are rusty." Daniel parked next to her car, one of the few left in the lot. "Assuming I ever had any in the first place."

"If not skill, per se, definitely potential." Sure, he used to annoy the crap out of her, but did he know there'd also been times when he'd made her knees weak and her stomach quiver? "I fantasized about you once or twice during Dr. Leonard's lectures."

Even in the dim lighting, Daniel's wide-eyed gape was obvious. But he recovered quickly. "What kind of fantasies?" His voice was silky, coaxing.

"Maybe I'll tell you. Someday."

The air between them crackled. His intent expression was heady, the thrill that shot through her even more delicious than plantain s'mores. Self-preservation had her climbing out of the car before she did something crazy. *Like front-seat sex in the office parking lot*?

It was a beautiful, clear winter night. An impressive number of stars twinkled down on them despite the city's lights. Shoving her hands in the pockets of her coat, she sat on the hood of her car and took a moment to appreciate the view. Daniel joined her, standing with his elbow against the hood. How would he react if she grabbed the lapels of his jacket and pulled him in for a kiss?

"Flirting lesson number one," she said lightly. "If a woman admits you've starred in her fantasies, she's probably interested."

His mouth curved in a sensual smile. "Probably?"

Damn, he had a great mouth. For all that she'd scoffed at him in the past about being an unimaginative rule follower, he had full lips more reminiscent of sweaty carnal weekends than stuffy classroom lectures.

"Gaze can be a good indication of desire," she murmured. Had he noticed her staring? "If a woman's uncomfortable, she might glance around for exits or possible rescue. If she's attracted, there's often a lot of eye contact."

He leaned close enough for her to breathe in peppermint and the faint, pleasant scent of sandalwood soap. "And if she's looking at my lips like she wants to taste them?"

So, yeah, he'd noticed. Since she was busted anyway, she gave in to impulse and traced his bottom lip with her finger. He shuddered out a breath, warm on her skin, his pupils dilated in dark contrast to his silvery eyes.

Her own breathing was unsteady as she slid her hand down his chest. "Go with your instincts."

With a sound that was part sigh, part groan, he cupped the nape of her neck and bent toward her. He traced her lips, as she had his, but with his tongue, teasing, enticing, before he angled his head and deepened their kiss, thrusting into her mouth. A jolt went through her, like a small static-electricity shock without the sting. This was pure pleasure.

She'd entertained dozens of naughty thoughts about Daniel Keegan, yet she'd never believed she would actually be in his arms, hungrily kissing him. It had been worth the wait. He wasn't just good at this; he was wickedly skilled, setting off hot prickling need through her body. Her knees fell to either side as he stepped closer, breaking their kiss to scrape his teeth over the column of her throat. Clutching his shoulders, she tilted her head to give him better access. He supported her with one strong arm behind her back.

His other hand had pushed aside her jacket and was

sliding over the slope of her breast. She closed her eyes as he palmed her through the layers of clothing. Aching desire built, her nipples hard and seeking attention. He stroked one with his thumb, and she tugged him close for a frantic kiss. When he pinched the sensitive peak, his mouth muffled her involuntary cry. It was all she could do not to pull him across her and have sex right there on the hood of her—

"What do you kids— Oh…" A man cleared his throat as a beam of light hit Mia's face.

She blinked, dazed by sensation and confused by the disembodied voice. Daniel was much quicker to react. While she was still mentally processing that they'd been interrupted by the night security guard who patrolled the property, Daniel had already straightened, tugging her wrist to pull her off of the car and partially behind him. He stood between her and the glare of the flashlight.

The stout security guard sounded as flustered as she felt. "Mistook you for a couple of teenagers. You shouldn't be here." Suddenly, he rocked back on his heels. *"Ms. Hayes?"*

It wasn't uncommon for her to work late hours, and the guard had offered to walk her to her car on more than one occasion. She raised her hand in a limp wave. "Hey, Myron."

He locked his gaze on the pavement, stammering, "I, ah…"

"We were just saying good-night," Daniel said. "We'll be on our way now."

Myron's head bobbed in relieved agreement. "Good,

good. Y'all drive safe." He got back into the little golf cart he used to cover the spacious lot.

Mia pulled her trench coat tight across her body, feeling exposed. But it occurred to her that Myron hadn't really seen anything other than some intense kissing. Nobody had been undressed. *Yet*. Now that she'd had a chance to regain her composure, she was able to see humor in being mistaken for a couple of kids necking.

She turned toward Daniel, a small smile tugging at the corner of her mouth. "Well, that was—"

"Unacceptable." His tone was grim. Bordering on angry.

Unacceptable? Not what a girl hoped to hear after a first kiss. The last of the pleasure she'd felt faded, making her newly aware of how cold the night had become.

"I apologize for my behavior." He shoved a hand through his hair. "That wasn't me. I *never*— You…"

She started to point out he hadn't acted alone, but maybe that was the point. Was he blaming her for their kisses? Why was he even upset? *He* wasn't the one who'd have to face Myron again. She stared, trying to understand what Daniel was feeling. But his expression was shuttered. He looked nothing like the playful man she'd spent the evening with.

Because he's reverted to form. Right now, he bore entirely too much resemblance to the remote, critical classmate who'd tried to shame her for her actions in the past. One would never guess by looking at him that he'd been aroused.

His voice was downright impersonal as he asked, "Are you okay to drive?"

"Fine." She'd been temporarily dazed, not drunk. That haze of desire she'd experienced was embarrassing next to Daniel's calm clarity when they'd been interrupted. While she'd been writhing against the car and losing her mind, had he been unaffected? No, not unaffected, not with the way he'd kissed her. But he hardly seemed swept away by passion.

He looked like a man who faulted her for his temporary loss of dignity. *That wasn't me,* he'd said. *You...* Sure. Why not wash his hands of all responsibility and dump it on her? An unpleasant sense of déjà vu stung her chest like heartburn. Why couldn't grown men be accountable for their own actions?

Teeth clenched, she unlocked her car door. "Good night, Daniel."

He hesitated, and she willed him to say something— anything—that made her feel like he didn't regret what they'd shared, that she hadn't been the only one caught up in the moment. Instead, he nodded stiffly. "Night."

Inside her car, she let loose a few choice expletives before putting the vehicle in reverse. *That was a humiliating end to the evening.*

It could have been worse, though. At least he'd delivered her back to her car after dinner and hadn't driven her home. Because, if they'd been in proximity of a bed and he'd kissed her like that... Given the disdainful way he'd eyed her after making out, she could just imagine how charming he'd be after they slept together.

Forget the question of whether he'd respect her in the morning—he barely respected her *now*.

Past college fantasies be damned, sex with Daniel Keegan was out of the question.

4

"WHAT THE HELL, Keegan?" Eli scowled. Across the court, Sean's teammate jogged after the basketball. "Were you aiming *anywhere* near the basket?"

They were playing two-on-two, but given Daniel's performance, Eli might have been better off taking on the other team alone.

Sounding more concerned than annoyed, Eli asked, "What's with you this morning? Lack of caffeine?"

In order to have the campus gym to themselves, they met at five forty-five. Sean declared it an unholy hour, but the time didn't bother Daniel. Since his insomnia problems had started, he was always out of bed by five anyway. Today, he'd jolted awake around four, pulled from scorching hot dreams of Mia and the kisses they'd shared last night.

In his dreams, there had been no security guard. And no stopping.

He'd awakened sexually frustrated, which was no less than he deserved, and still furious with himself.

After a lifetime of prioritizing proper behavior, he'd let the lure of Mia's mouth turn him into a ravening beast. He hadn't spared a second's concern for whether someone would see them or how that could affect her. They'd been right outside her place of business, for God's sake. *What were you thinking?*

The beam of the guard's flashlight had sliced through the night like an accusation. Daniel had recoiled immediately, running on autopilot as a hundred lectures from his parents rang in his ears. He'd been so chagrined over his undisciplined behavior that he could hardly recall what he'd said to Mia. He did remember her stricken expression, though—the one she'd tried to hide before climbing into her car. She must think he was a total ass, no better than the men she'd described who groped and pawed at women.

"Sorry," Daniel said. "Been distracted lately." *Lately* meaning since last night, and *distracted* meaning he was unable to concentrate on a damn thing besides Mia's enthusiasm and the heat of her mouth.

Eli knelt to tighten his shoelaces. "Still obsessing about the committee recommendation? You know the provost's in your corner. I get that waiting sucks, but the decision's in the hands of the president and the board of regents now. Don't make yourself crazy in the meantime."

Tenure. Right. That goal he'd busted his ass to attain. "Actually, work was the furthest thing from my mind."

Eli stood, his expression perplexed.

What did it say about Daniel's life that his friends

assumed his career was the only thing he had going for him? "I had a date last night. Dinner with Mia."

"No kidding? That's fantas—"

Daniel grimaced.

"Not fantastic?"

"Actually, it was. Until the very end. I…" *…fell on her like a sex-starved maniac?* They'd been only a few feet from passing traffic, and he'd gone for second base like a horny teenager. Lord knew what he would have done without Myron's fortuitous interruption. "I screwed up."

"Hey!" Sean dribbled the ball, scowling at them. "Considering the embarrassing score, I get the need to talk strategy. But could we return to our game sometime before spring break?"

"Surprised you're in such a hurry to give up your lead," Eli called back. "Might as well savor it while you've still got it. Ready, Daniel?"

He nodded.

"FYI," Eli added under his breath, "I've screwed up a time or two with Bex. In my experience, flowers help."

"Thanks." But Daniel doubted an assortment of plant life was going to make up for his boorish behavior.

"Now focus. Quit throwing away your shots."

Unfortunately, Daniel couldn't shake the feeling he already had—not on the basketball court, but with the sexy-as-hell event coordinator. She'd given him a look of near loathing before she'd driven away.

He wasn't sure what he could say to convince her

to ever go out with him again. Considering his wildly undisciplined reaction to her, maybe it was best if he stayed away from her. Kept his distance. It was sound logic, but on some primal level, he rejected the idea even as he had it. Never kiss Mia again? Never touch her?

With an inward snarl, he lunged for Sean to steal the ball, knocking his friend on his ass.

Sean grunted a surprised expletive before propping himself up on his elbow. "Foul."

Eli fought a smile. "Dude, I said 'focus,' not 'maim.'"

"Right. Sorry. I lost my head for a moment." *A moment? Ha.* He hadn't felt like himself since Mia turned around at that bachelor party, meeting his gaze. Avoiding her might be the only way to return to normal.

Screw normal. The restless part of him he habitually stifled refused to stay silent. Maybe it was time to admit he didn't want "normal." He wanted change. He wanted excitement. And he desperately wanted Mia Hayes.

"Brant is *perfect*," Wren gushed as she unrolled her mat along the studio wall. "Well, perfect for me, anyway."

Mia and her friend Wren Kendrick had driven to the Tuesday night yoga class together. Wren managed an upscale lingerie store and occasionally gave Mia a generous friends-and-family discount, which was how Mia happened to own the perfect corset and fishnets to work a burlesque party. Both women had been working so hard lately that girl time had been scarce; Mia had yet to meet Wren's new boyfriend. The bubbly blonde had been chatting about Brant nonstop for the past fifteen minutes. Hopefully, she'd wind down before class started. Otherwise, they were in for another evening of the instructor shooting Wren pointed glances. Talking was not encouraged during the ninety-minute session.

"I've never dated a man I have more in common with," Wren said.

"That's great," Mia murmured absently. She was glad for Wren's joy but running out of supportive things to interject in the conversation.

"Our personalities are just so in *sync*."

What must that be like? Annoyingly, Mia's mind drifted to Daniel. Again. He'd been in her thoughts way too much today—not that she believed for a moment that the preoccupation was mutual. He seemed to have wiped her from his mind before he even drove out of the parking lot. His expression had been so insultingly blank she'd wanted to shake his shoulders. *Hi, remember me? Mia? You just had your tongue in my mouth?*

Their sizzling kisses might support the generalization of opposites attracting, but she had too much self-respect to share a hot night with a man likely to sneer at her the next morning. Whatever had motivated his stated need for change, modifications to a person's lifestyle or behavior were often fleeting.

Like temporary insanity. *That's what you experienced, a little hormone-driven insanity.* Nothing to obsess over.

It was embarrassing how distracted she'd been today. Thank goodness she'd been able to avoid Shannon and any perceptive questions about Mia's mood. A dental appointment had kept the woman out of the office that morning, and Mia had been on the go all afternoon. Yoga was the perfect opportunity to regain clarity and perspective. She straightened her legs in front of her, stretching over them as Wren continued her ecstatic Brant-themed babbling.

"You know the first time you have sex with someone and he doesn't know what you like yet, so you're trying to gently steer him toward what you want without seeming bossy?"

Mia made a noncommittal sound. She spoke her mind, in bed and out of it, and had never much worried about whether she sounded bossy. What would Daniel be like in the bedroom? Willing to follow his lover's lead, or convinced his way was the right one, just as he had been in college? *Stop it.* At twenty, she may have fantasized once or twice about the opportunity to help loosen him up, but she was an adult now. She didn't have time in her life for a man who wouldn't appreciate her.

"My sisters are scandalized I slept with Brant after knowing him less than a week," Wren said, unconcerned that the woman one mat over was shamelessly eavesdropping, "but it didn't *feel* like our first time. It was like we'd known each other forever, like we were two halves of the same whole."

Typical Wren. She lived—and loved—boldly. Where Shannon was shy and reserved in her personal life, Wren liked to jump in with both feet. Mia couldn't imagine ever declaring a guy her other half after a handful of dates, but she respected her friend's optimistic courage. "I hope he—"

"Good evening, ladies." The instructor walked into the room.

Hallelujah. Time to begin. Mia wasn't really in the right headspace to gush about Wren's new love, even though that was bitchy of her. If things had gone differently last night, Wren would be the first to cheer for her. *If things had gone differently…* Her imagination started down that path, but she ruthlessly yanked it back as the class opened their session with a collective "Om."

For about an hour, she was able to push Daniel Keegan from her mind. But toward the end of the session, they went into yin practice, which involved long-held poses and encouraged meditation. It gave her entirely too much time to think. Plus, after sixty minutes of focusing so intently on her body, on her breathing, on the pleasant soreness of muscles as she challenged herself… Well, it only made sense that her thoughts were lured back to the sensual experience of being pressed against Daniel's body, who'd made her breathing uneven and her skin tingle.

She could tell herself all day long that he didn't deserve her, but she couldn't help wondering, if the chance to kiss him again arose, how would she resist? *By remembering how aloof he was afterward.* Almost as good as a cold shower. She wanted a lover who ran hot. Who looked at her with enough yearning to make her shiver. Who craved her unashamedly.

Daniel Keegan was not that man—not based on the evidence of last night.

But heaven help her if he ever got comfortable with his passionate side. Because there'd be no resisting him then.

"Must've been some date Monday." Shannon flashed a smile over the top of her coffee mug.

Mia froze in the act of removing her coat. "Why do you say that?" She hadn't pegged Myron as the type who would blab about what he'd seen to other people in the building, but maybe she'd been wrong.

Shannon pointed toward the reception desk. "Because, flowers. You obviously made an impression."

"Uh-huh." A slight impression of her butt on the front of her car, maybe. Yet she crossed the room in three long strides to read the card, her curiosity piqued. Given his almost robotic goodbye, she hadn't expected any further contact from Daniel, much less contact in the form of a square vase filled with carnations, white roses and delicate purple filler flowers.

The note was terse. *I'm sorry. Daniel.*

For which part, exactly? Asking her to dinner in the first place? Kissing her? Or was he apologizing for Myron's bad timing?

With a sigh, she crumpled the card.

Shannon's eyebrows shot skyward. "Dare I ask?"

"I want to discuss my date with Daniel about as much as you want to discuss your progress with Paige."

"Wow. That bad, huh?"

"Any messages?" Mia asked, officially changing the subject.

They discussed clients and the day's schedule while Mia fixed her own cup of coffee, although she doubted caffeine was a good idea given her already antsy state of mind. She needed to call Penelope Wainwright this morning, and she needed to be at her most professional when she spoke to the affluent woman. No sense sniping at their biggest client or sounding scattered because she was busy trying to decipher a bouquet of flowers.

Shannon returned to her desk, nodding at the arrangement. "Do you want these in your office?"

"No. Find a place for them out here that isn't inconvenient for you. They brighten up the lobby."

"Got it." She hesitated, her expression apologetic. "Do you want me to put him through or take a message if he calls?"

She thought about his withdrawn manner, the perfunctory message on the card. "He won't."

GLANCING FROM THE stack of tests on his desk to the clock on the wall, Daniel felt a tug of dread in the pit of his stomach. "You have officially overextended yourself," he muttered. In addition to the classes he taught and the articles he was scheduled to publish this year, he'd signed on for some extra volunteer activities, hoping they'd help him stand out as a tenure candidate. He was the faculty advisor for two student clubs and was serving on the curriculum review committee which met every Wednesday. In ten minutes, as a matter of fact.

Grade faster.

When his office phone rang, his first impulse was to let the call go to voice mail. He didn't have time to talk to anyone. But what if it was Mia? She should've received the flowers by now, so she could be calling to thank him.

He grabbed for the phone, almost fumbling the receiver. "Professor Keegan speaking."

"Daniel?"

"Felicity." He was shocked to hear her voice; he was also a little stunned to realize she hadn't even crossed his mind in the past two days. His thoughts had been too full of Mia. "How are you? Wait, I should let you know, I have a meeting to get to in a few minutes." When he abruptly ended the call, he didn't want her to take it personally.

"I'm fine, thanks. And this won't take long. I just wanted to let you know I won't be at the wedding this weekend. I RSVPed yes before the holidays, but obviously that was when I'd planned to be your date."

"Felicity, you don't have to cancel because of me." Running into her was no longer the awkward proposition it would have been a week ago. Not just because he'd gone out with someone else but because his response to Mia had helped demonstrate that his relationship with Felicity had lacked passion. "Eli and Bex are your friends, too." The four of them had double-dated often, spent holiday weekends together, celebrated promotions and other milestones.

"And I wish them every happiness. It's Rebekah's big day. I want her to be able to focus on that, not worried about any confrontations between us."

He almost laughed. Neither he nor Felicity were the type for angry confrontations. "I trust us to be cordial. Maybe even friends, eventually." Down the road, once his pride had fully recovered and he was no longer worried that friendship between them would give their manipulative families false hope. "After all, we've known each other for most of our lives."

"Friends," she echoed. "Then you aren't mad at me for breaking up with you?"

"No. I wish you'd told me sooner that you were unhappy, but I'm not mad."

"I…" She chose her words carefully, haltingly. "I wasn't unhappy, exactly. I care a lot about you. We had a very comfortable relationship built on mutual respect. It just…wasn't enough."

"Yeah. I get that." His scandal-phobic family, still reeling from the antics of his infamous uncle, had always encouraged Daniel to live a muted existence, but why should Felicity settle for that? *Why should I?* "Look, I really have to get to this meeting, but please know that you're welcome at the wedding if you change your mind."

"Thank you."

He hung up the phone thinking half a dozen things at once—from wondering whether he'd convinced her to attend the wedding to being relieved that hearing her voice hadn't hurt. But his strongest reaction was disappointment that it hadn't been Mia on the other end. He made himself a deal as he caught the elevator downstairs: if Mia hadn't gotten in touch by the time his committee meeting ended, he would call her.

They'd had a lot of fun during dinner the other night. Yes, he'd screwed up the last twenty minutes of the date, but if Eli was right about flowers smoothing over social gaffes, maybe Mia would be willing to see him again.

Curriculum meetings were long and boring. Daniel usually resented the intrusion on his schedule. But leaning back in his chair and imagining the best-case scenarios of his upcoming conversation with Mia made it the most enjoyable hour of his day.

As IT TURNED OUT, Shannon needn't have worried about what to do if Daniel called the office phone because he called Mia's cell phone directly. When she saw his name on the caller display, she briefly considered ignoring him to continue the email she was typing. *Avoidance is the coward's way out.*

With a sigh, she hit the accept button. "Hello," she said flatly.

"Hi. It's Daniel. I, uh… Did you get the flowers I sent?"

"I did." What she didn't get was *why*. What were they supposed to accomplish? "They add a nice splash of color to the office."

"Good."

A long pause stretched between them, an almost expectant silence. If she'd opened solitaire on her computer, she could be halfway through a game by now. "Thank you for the flowers, Daniel." Was that why he'd called, to give her the opportunity to express socially mandated gratitude? If so, mission accomplished. Now he could go away. "But I have a lot to do and—"

"I meant what I said in the card," he blurted. "I really am sorry."

She rolled her chair away from the desk and stood, agitated enough to pace. "Sorry for what, specifically?" If he said he regretted kissing her, she was hanging up on him.

"For my loss of control. We had a great evening, until I mauled you in a public place. Not even a romantic place—a parking lot overlooking the street."

Though she might tout the importance of ambience to her clients, in Mia's opinion, geography wasn't what made a moment romantic. She and Daniel had created their own mood.

When her lap around the office took her by the window, she tugged the blinds closed, not wanting to stare out at the parking lot and relive the pleasure. "It was only a few kisses," she said, her casual tone belying how aroused she'd been. She'd been feverish with wanting his hands on her body. "Hardly a legitimate mauling."

"Still, it was disrespectful to you. I can't remember the last time I was so furious with myself."

Her breath caught as she reinterpreted his expression after Myron left. He'd seemed so full of scathing disdain—but it hadn't been aimed at her. "None of it was because of me?"

"Oh, honey, what happened was *definitely* because of you." His voice was thick with praise, not blame.

"Because of how sexy you are, because of how kissing you made me forget myself."

A thrill shot through her, bringing back all the old fantasies about corrupting him. Hypocritical fantasies, she realized now. Because as much fun as it might have been to imagine being a bad influence, just between two people should be equal. She didn't want to be an excuse for a man's actions. It skirted too closely to the memory of her parents' disapproval. *Are you sure you didn't do something to encourage him?*

She expelled a breath, leaving the past where it belonged. "For the record, you are quite the kisser, too. And you don't owe me an apology—not for that part, anyway. The way you behaved afterward was a little insulting, though. You were so..."

"Standoffish? Stern?" He gave a humorless chuckle. "The Keegan DNA at work. I've been on the receiving end of it many times. I'm so—"

"Don't say you're sorry again. It's not necessary," she added, softening her tone.

"Then you forgive me?"

"Yes."

"Enough to join me tomorrow night for the campus concert series?" he pressed. "There's an orchestra—"

"No, thank you."

"It's not as boring as it sounds. They're doing a selection of—"

"I don't think classical music is boring. Not all of it, anyway. I just don't think it's a good idea for us to see each other again."

He'd just pointed out that he was subject to "the

Keegan DNA." Moments of aloof reserve like Monday night's were hardwired into him. He'd turned out to be a far more entertaining dinner companion than she'd anticipated, but that didn't mean he would ever be comfortable with public displays of affection or spontaneous acts. She could think of a hundred ways she might offend his sensibilities without even trying.

"Oh." He sounded wounded, but only for a split second. Then he rallied, a smile in his voice. "So we won't see each other, then. Except for at the wedding rehearsal Friday. And again at the ceremony this weekend."

"Those are different."

"Those are opportunities. Maybe I'll change your mind about me."

"You won't." But her tone lacked conviction.

"I should let you get back to work. See you soon, Mia."

Damn if her pulse didn't pick up at the prospect. "Goodbye, Daniel."

Emotions mixed, she disconnected the phone.

It rang again less than five minutes later, and she forced herself not to grin at his name on the screen. "Weird," she said in greeting. "I would have thought you were too straitlaced to be a stalker."

"I have a birthday coming up," he reminded her. "How do you know I'm not calling in a professional capacity?"

"Oh. Is this a business call?"

"Nah, I'm stalking you—but only for the good of the planet."

"What exactly did you put in your coffee today, Professor?"

"Hear me out. We both have to go to the rehearsal anyway, right? And I know Bex invited you to the dinner afterward."

"She did." Mia had appreciated the generosity, but pointed out that including the wedding coordinator as a guest wasn't necessary. Bex had teasingly asked since when either of them cared about convention.

"Well, since we're both going to the same places, don't you think we should carpool? It's the environmentally friendly thing to do," he said with mock solemnity.

His playful side was difficult to resist. But which version of him would show up Friday night—Mr. Irresistible or Dr. Keegan?

"Daniel, Monday night was a lot of fun. Until it wasn't." She understood his behavior better now, but it had been such a slap in the face after the heated intimacy they'd shared. "I just don't know what to expect from you."

"Oh, the irony that Mia Hayes could find *me* unpredictable." He lowered his voice to a conspiratorial whisper. "I'll let you in on a secret—I'm stuffy and humdrum."

His kisses were the fiery opposite of humdrum. Anticipation quickened through her. *If you're his date Friday night,* the little devil on her shoulder whispered, *you'll get to kiss him again.* With no security guard in sight, who knew where those kisses might lead? There was no counterargument from a shoulder angel; Mia's angel had gone on a coffee break years ago and never returned.

"Can you pick me up at my apartment at six?" she asked.

"No problem. My last class of the day ends at three thirty. And, Mia? You won't regret this." His husky tone was even more of a promise than his words, a sensual guarantee that feathered up her spine in tiny shivers.

Suddenly she was counting the hours until six o'clock on Friday.

5

THE FIRST TIME Daniel had been assigned to work a group project with Mia in college had been excruciating. Not only had he struggled with an unwelcome attraction to her, her flirting with the other group member when they should have been working made Daniel worry she was flighty and a threat to his grade. But no one who watched her now, overseeing the details of the wedding rehearsal, could ever mistake her for flighty.

She was organized and efficient, cheerful but with an underlying steel that made it clear anyone who didn't follow instructions would face consequences. Her talents were particularly useful in dealing with Rebekah's parents, who were divorced and disliked being in the same room. Mia was a polite but firm buffer, keeping their bickering to a minimum and ensuring that no one upset the bride-to-be.

Bex and Eli weren't having a church wedding. They were getting married in a solarium that, one hundred years ago, had been a two-building hospital ward for children. Its community history resonated with Bex, and the space was beautiful, with its high ceilings and gleaming hardwood floors. For now, the sun had set, but tomorrow afternoon, light would pour through the many windows. In preparation for the ceremony and subsequent reception, Mia was coordinating with florists, caterers, and the trustees who maintained and rented out the property.

Daniel was impressed with her ability to juggle it all and a little turned on by her take-charge attitude. Frankly, everything about her was turning him on, from the smile she'd flashed him when she'd opened her apartment door earlier to the leather straps of her shoes peeking out from beneath her slacks. She was in professional mode tonight, wearing a comparatively restrained sweater with her hair secured in some kind of elegant twist, but the high heels and her bold red lipstick added a hint of naughtiness. He found every detail delectable.

And he didn't delude himself that he was hiding his admiration from anyone.

Although Eli and Bex were too caught up in each other and their impending big day to pay much attention, Sean—who was serving as an usher along with one of Eli's cousins—was openly smirking. And Eli's mom, who had always been fond of Daniel, had given him an encouraging thumbs-up behind Mia's back, obviously approving of his good taste.

He was so preoccupied watching Mia, appreciating the curve of her breasts beneath the filmy knit of her sweater and the curve of her smile as she joked with

Bex, that he missed what Mia was saying. When she harrumphed in his general direction, he realized she'd been explaining where he should stand. He quickly took his mark, flashing her a sheepish grin in apology.

Once the rehearsal ended and they were in his car on the way to dinner, she chided him for his poor listening skills.

"I hope your students pay better attention than you do." She crossed her arms in a way that made her cleavage even more stunning, and he fought to keep his eyes on the road. "You completely tuned me out."

"Not exactly." Mia had been uppermost in his mind; he just hadn't been able to focus on her explanations of musical cues and ceremonial candle lightings. "I was busy imagining all the things I'd want to do to you if we were alone."

"Oh." A slow smile spread across her face. "Do share."

But they were already pulling into the restaurant parking lot, so he echoed her mischievous taunt from the other night, "Maybe I'll tell you. Someday."

The Moroccan restaurant had been the site of Eli's first date with Bex. The location was both sentimental and practical, since it was just a couple of blocks from the wedding venue. A dark-haired hostess in a jewel-toned tunic asked them to remove their shoes, then led them to a private, candlelit dining room.

About half of the guests had already arrived and were now seated on plump, richly colored cushions. The sensual surroundings made Daniel wish more than ever that he and Mia were alone. As a longtime friend of Eli's, Daniel knew most everyone here. Mia was theoretically the outsider, yet she was greeted with as many friendly waves and hellos as he was. It was a little surprising that the brash young woman he'd once known had become such a people-person. He'd heard her claim before that she didn't give a damn what others thought of her, yet she'd developed the enviable skill of putting others at ease.

As people around them placed drink orders, Daniel murmured, "You are impressive on many levels."

Mia beamed. "I like to think so. But just so we're having the same conversation, what brought on the praise?"

"The way you interact with everyone, as if you're genuinely fascinated by them."

"I am, mostly. I mean, I once considered faking narcolepsy to get out of talking to a guy intent on selling me insurance, but in general… I'm intrigued by how different we all are while sharing such fundamental similarities. I like being around people." Her smile was tinged with sympathy. "Whereas *you* are miserable and have fought the urge to check your watch twice already."

Shit, he was a terrible best man. Maybe he should slip the watch off and keep it in his pocket until after dinner. "I am thrilled for Eli and I'm happy to be here—"

Her grin widened, silently calling him a liar yet giving him credit for the effort.

"I just don't like large groups. It's a minor rebellion on my part. Keegans are raised to be social."

"Uh-huh. From the little I know about your family, I can't imagine they urged you to be some kind of party animal."

Political party, maybe. "Oh, I wasn't supposed to have anything as sincere and straightforward as fun." He was surprised by the depth of bitterness in his voice. He almost never allowed himself to complain to anyone but Eli about his family—and even that was rare. "I was taught that in a gathering like this, I should network with as many people as possible, quickly identifying how each one might be of use to me."

Mia let out a low whistle. "Your parents sound like a hoot and a half. You *must* introduce us sometime."

Imagining his parents trying to handle Mia with their usual tight-smiled superficiality made him laugh out loud. They wouldn't know what hit them. "That's a very tempting idea—definite spectator appeal—but I like you too much to inflict them on you."

She wiggled on her cushion, scooting closer until her legs brushed his and vanilla-scented lotion teased him, making him want to taste her skin. "I like you, too."

Despite his typical unease in group settings, he was grinning like an idiot when the waitress brought their drinks and an appetizer of lentil and chickpea soup. By the time the empty bowls were cleared away, Daniel was actually enjoying himself. He listened as Mia chatted with a woman across from them, a microbiologist with surprisingly funny lab anecdotes. Daniel contributed periodically but mostly relaxed and let himself savor Mia's company. She'd tucked her legs to the side and was leaning into him as if their closeness was perfectly natural, making his prior existence seem sterile and stilted in contrast.

Mia was so comfortable in her own skin, comfortable showing physical affection, unlike anyone in the Keegan family. Well, except for disgraced Uncle Truman, who'd lost his senatorial race due to newspaper photos of him being affectionate. With three prostitutes at once. It was that scandal which had spawned the family philosophy of repressing vices and desires.

Had Daniel, a product of that stifled background, completely overreacted to their make-out session in the parking lot Monday? What had Mia said? *Only a few kisses, hardly a legitimate mauling.* From her more liberal point of view, his response no doubt seemed ridiculous. Thank God she'd given him a second chance. He desperately wanted to kiss her again. *You want to do a lot more than that.* He shifted uncomfortably, glad for the napkin that concealed his lap.

"Mmm." Mia gave him a knowing look, her eyes twinkling with an answering hunger. "Penny for your thoughts."

He leaned close enough to whisper his confession but lightly bit her earlobe first, loving the tremor that ran through her, the catch in her breathing. "I'm sorry I was an uptight jerk about the security guard busting us. If I had it all to do again, I'd wave Myron on his way and go back to kissing you with the attention you deserve."

"Really?" Her hazel eyes widened fractionally, as if she were impressed.

Impressing Mia Hayes was a heady, addictive sensation. He wanted to watch those eyes go heavy-lidded with desire, wanted to hear her voice turn husky with approval over the story he spun. At this precise moment, it felt less like a playful exaggeration and more like the truth. As if he *was* the kind of man who would kiss her senseless with no care for the rest of the world. There was only him and Mia.

He kept his voice low, cupping the nape of her bare neck. "I'd remove your top and your bra, watch your nipples grow even harder in the cold." His gaze fell to her lips, pausing at the delicate hollow of her throat before dropping to her breasts.

"Careful, Professor." Her tone was taut with need. "I might just hold you to that."

Damn, he hoped so. "They're sensitive, aren't they? Your breasts?" Her eager nod was liberating, spurring him on. "I'd trace light circles across them, coming closer and closer to the center, but I wouldn't touch your nipples. Not until you begged me to. I'd lay you back on the hood of that car and make you crazy for me."

Beneath the table, she raked her fingers over his thigh with enough force that he felt the scrape of her nails through his clothes. It took every ounce of self-discipline not to reach for her hand and place it over his throbbing erection. She skated just near enough for him to suck in an audible breath; the couple on his other side probably heard. Daniel didn't care.

He slid his hand down her spine. "You are a very dangerous woman."

"Complaining?"

"Hell, no. Dangerous women are my favorite kind." As of right now.

Whatever response she meant to make faded as she caught sight of the servers approaching with the second course. They set pies down in the center of each table.

Daniel was surprised at the sugar and cinnamon dusting the top of the pastries. "Seems pretty early in the meal for dessert."

She grinned. "My kind of place. Dessert early and often, I say."

But as he tried his first bite, he realized that it wasn't really a dessert. It was a savory chicken pie in a light, flaky dough, the sweet notes an odd but intriguing contrast.

"Not what I expected," Mia said, echoing his thoughts.

"Disappointed?" The woman did love her desserts.

"No." She met his eyes. "Sometimes the best things turn out to be quite different than what you were expecting. I like surprises."

A week ago, Daniel would have said he did not. But Mia had changed that. The chemistry between them was intense, different from anything he'd experienced before, and he couldn't safely predict where it would lead. But he couldn't wait to find out.

WHEN BEX'S MAID of honor laughingly grabbed Mia's hand and tugged her onto the floor, where one of the restaurant's belly dancers was giving an impromptu lesson, Mia went willingly. Not just because she wanted to be a good sport for Bex and Eli, but because she was restless. Fidgety from an hour and a half of sitting next to Daniel, overwhelmed by his unique brand of seduction.

Leave it to a lit professor to use his words so effectively. Unlike some of her past dates, Daniel hadn't jumped straight to a physical onslaught. He wooed her with that deep voice. She almost envied the students who got to listen to him for an hour at a time, wondering how many of them harbored "Hot for Teacher" crushes.

As much as she loved Daniel's voice, what she loved most was the gravelly growl that crept into his tone, the one that said he was struggling to keep control of himself. *He's not alone.* Did he know how wet she was after ninety minutes of banter and innuendo and sensual promises about what they would do to each other in the very near future?

A woman to her left jostled her, and Mia tried to return her concentration to the beginner belly-dancing moves being demonstrated. But how could she focus when she could feel Daniel's hot, hungry gaze on her? Suddenly, she wasn't part of a giggling group of women sharing a moment of camaraderie; his palpable lust isolated her. She was a dancer performing for an audience of one. She rolled her hips for him, slowing her arm movements to a sinuous stretch. He leaned forward, expression so intent that she almost faltered. It was difficult to be graceful with thick need running through her veins.

As Mia returned to the table, the waitstaff was clearing away the last of the plates. Which meant it was time to go. *Now what?* She didn't think she'd make it through the night without Daniel inside her. But she had mixed feelings about inviting him into her apartment. After so many pent-up fantasies, she wasn't sure she could pull herself away from him before dawn, and she needed a decent night's sleep. Tomorrow was Rebekah's perfect day, and it was Mia's job to insure that perfection.

Daniel helped her into her coat, then laced his fingers through hers. "I can't invite you back to my place—Eli's bunking there tonight—but I'm not ready to say goodbye yet. What about you?"

She shook her head mutely.

He rubbed a thumb over the heel of her palm, gliding down to the pulse point in her wrist, the caress making her warm and tingly. She'd teased him before about old-fashioned gallantry, but who knew there was an art to hand-holding? He made it a sexy prelude, and she almost couldn't breathe past her hunger to feel his caresses everywhere else.

When they said good-night to Eli and Bex at the door, Daniel double-checked that his friend had his spare key. "Make yourself comfortable," he said. "I'll be back later. Mia and I just wanted to visit the campus first. For nostalgia's sake."

She waited until they'd stepped outside to ask, "We wanted to visit the campus?" That was news to her, but she didn't care where they went.

"It seemed like a good idea," he said, his breath a visible puff in the cold air. "Beautiful night for a walk."

"It's freezing."

"It's invigorating." He tugged her against his side. "Besides, I promise to keep you warm."

And just like that, meandering across campus on a chilly January night seemed like a brilliant plan. "Deal."

As he started the car, he asked, "Have you been back to the college since graduating?"

She shook her head. "Launching my company has kept me crazy-busy, and there was never any real reason to." Did she have a reason now? The thought of visiting him sometime was pleasant. Maybe in the spring, when the weather was nice, she could stop by with a picnic lunch and— *In the spring?* She did a double take at her assumption that she'd be in a visiting mood months from now. Until tonight, she and Daniel had barely even made it through a single evening without things going sideways…and the night wasn't over yet. Bex and Eli's wedding had thrown them together, but only for the moment. *So enjoy the moment.*

When the clock tower at the center of campus came into view, she was surprised by an unexpected pull of nostalgia. "I wish I'd…been in a better mood when I went to college."

"What, you registered for the wrong classes because you were cranky that day?"

Cranky was a mild word for it. "I was angry at my parents when I moved out. My dad, mostly. We fought most of my senior year." It seemed like too much of a downer to tell Daniel about the divorced man she used to babysit for and how he'd made a pass at— No, *as-*

saulted her. She refused to downplay it the way her parents had when she'd gone to them, scared and outraged, needing some kind of justice. Some kind of assurance that the actions of a drunken man twice her age weren't her fault.

"Anyway." She looked out the window, hoping she sounded appropriately nonchalant about the distant past. "I left home with a chip on my shoulder, and I let it color my college experience." Then again, college had also been where she'd laid the foundation for her future and joined the intern program that ultimately led to her doing what she loved. "But it wasn't all bad."

"Of course not. You were lucky enough to meet *me*."

She laughed, her pensive mood dispelled. "The highlight of my university years," she deadpanned.

They'd reached a gated faculty parking lot, and Daniel rolled down his window to swipe the ID card that had been hanging from his rearview mirror. "For me, college was an escape."

"From your family?"

"From attention."

She snorted indelicately. "Oh, please. Mr. I-have-an-answer-for-every-question Teacher's Pet? You sought out plenty of attention."

"Getting noticed because you can list the conflicting use of storms in Shakespeare's plays is a lot different than being noticed because you're a Keegan." After a moment he added, "I've long since realized that, contrary to my mother's paranoia, the entire world is *not* watching us like we're the Kennedys or the royal family. But in the community where I was raised, it felt true. My family was at the center of everything, and I left with an overdeveloped sense of importance."

"Guess that explains why you were such a pompous ass."

He flashed her a quick grin as he turned into a parking space. "While *you* were a ray of sweet-natured sunshine."

"I can be sweet when I want to be." Possibly.

"Ha!" He opened his door. "I'll believe it when I see it."

You and me both. "Maybe I'll surprise you."

"Of that, I have no doubt." The amusement was gone from his voice, replaced by...admiration? Wistfulness?

She climbed out of the car. "For the record, you are also full of surprises, Professor. The dirty talk at the restaurant, for instance." She felt almost shy bringing it up, which was ridiculous, given her often shocking vocabulary. He hadn't even been vulgar, just...specific. "That caught me off guard."

"Me, too," he admitted. His smile bordered on smug as he happily declared, "Completely inappropriate way for a Keegan to express himself."

They stepped up onto the sidewalk and she glanced around at the familiar landmarks. "So, where to?" she asked. "Student union to see if the coffee's as bad as I remember? The science building so we can reenact some of the arguments we had in Professor Leonard's class?"

"The coffee on campus has improved drastically. But I thought I'd show you my office."

"I can't believe you teach here. Doesn't it seem

like just yesterday we were attending classes? Now we're…" She grimaced. "Grown-ups."

"Okay, never mind showing you my office. Maybe we should just egg a couple of dorms and TP the trees on the mall."

If he wanted to misbehave, she had suggestions of her own. "There's always streaking."

"Mia. When you see me naked for the first time, it is *not* going to be in thirty-degree weather. Leave a man his pride."

The idea of seeing him undressed, exploring the hard planes of his lean body, left her giddy. *Yes, please.* She smirked. "You're so sure we're going to see each other naked?"

Stopping, he cupped her face with his hands, his smile devilishly cocky. "Very, very sure." He lowered his head toward hers. "And very soon."

6

EAGER FOR HIS KISS, Mia stretched up on her toes to meet him, heat thrumming through her as his mouth claimed hers. She'd been waiting for this moment all night, and now she was greedy for him.

Clutching the front of his jacket, she rubbed her tongue against his, going a little dizzy when he sucked it. His hands were splayed on her ass, holding her close enough to feel the rigid heat of his cock against her stomach. She wanted to curl her fingers around him, watch his eyes brighten with need, wanted to lick the length of him, swiping her tongue under the crown as if he were a wonderfully profane ice cream cone. *Do not reach for his zipper.* At least, not yet, on the sidewalk, in the shadow of one of the university's libraries.

She pried her lips from his long enough to ask, "Should we be doing this here? Not that it bothers me, but since this is where you work…" She was trying to show him the same consideration he'd given her when he'd apologized for necking in front of her office. "Are you worried about your reputation if anyone sees us?"

"Now that you mention it, I was planning to take you somewhere more private."

"Lead the way," she said, desire adding an impatient rasp to her voice.

He slid his hand in hers, his thumb making slow sweeps over the skin between her own thumb and forefinger. "Were you serious when you told me you had fantasies about me during Dr. Leonard's class?"

She narrowed her eyes. "Do I strike you as someone who says things I don't mean?"

"No, ma'am. Didn't mean to doubt you. I just…"

"I got annoyed during one of your presentations. The information was great, but the delivery was condescending. As if you weren't sure the rest of us mere mortals would be able to follow your genius explanations."

He winced. "Oh, well, when you explain it that way, I can totally understand why you'd be hot for me."

"I started thinking about how much fun it would be to rattle you, to interrupt your perfectly polished speech. So I considered flashing you."

"You what?"

She gave him an angelic smile, running a finger along the V of her neckline, tugging the material aside to give him a glimpse of cleavage. "It was such a satisfying visual image—grabbing the hem of my T-shirt, flipping it to my chin, showing you my tits. You, gaping in dumbstruck lust."

"I don't know whether I'm depressed it never happened or grateful. The sudden loss of blood from my brain could have permanently damaged my GPA." He reached for her hand, deliberately grazing her breast in the process, and pressed a kiss to her knuckles. "But flunking out might have been worth it."

"There were other fantasies, too." Heated ones. Her undeniable physical attraction to him had been a perversely potent combination with her dislike of him.

He'd seemed so aloof, which she'd taken as his thinking he was better than his peers. And he had been academically cocky. Looking back, she wondered if some of his attitude was loneliness she'd misinterpreted. His family hadn't been warm and affectionate; it wasn't surprising that someone afraid to let his guard down would have difficulty making friends.

"I considered asking your opinion on my tattoo," she admitted.

He cocked his head. "The feather?"

"No. The one you haven't seen yet."

His eyes glinted with interest, and his gaze dropped over her in a very focused perusal, as if he'd suddenly developed X-ray vision and would be able to spot the mystery tattoo through her clothes. Since it was on her inner thigh, she didn't think he was going to have much luck.

Giving up the search, he traced the feather on the back of her neck with an excruciatingly light touch, a whisper of tantalizing sensation against her skin. "So why a flaming feather?"

She made a face; the choice that had seemed inspired at eighteen struck her as less original now. "A phoenix feather to symbolize my newfound independence. Rising from unpleasant past incidents and recreating myself. Cliché, right?"

"You're talking to a literature professor. We thrive on unsubtle symbolism." He dragged his finger in another lazy outline of the ink. "Your tattoo used to drive me crazy when you wore your hair up. Like tonight. I think, subconsciously, I was dying to do this." He leaned forward to kiss her nape, biting gently. But not too gently. How did he know just how much pressure to use, just the right scalding sting to make her quiver for more without it hurting? "I made it a point never to sit behind you again after I got so distracted during a lecture that I had to borrow someone else's notes."

"Really?" This admission thrilled her, earning him another confession of her own. "I saw you jogging once. Without your shirt on. I was in the world's most boring Italian class, listening to a teacher with a voice like warm milk conjugate irregular verbs, and you passed by the window. You stopped for a drink at a water fountain, and I wondered what would happen if I walked right up to you and licked off the drop of sweat rolling down between your shoulder blades."

His grip tightened around her hand, and he tugged her along the sidewalk at a faster pace. "Any other fantasies?"

"Yes."

"Tell me." The gravelly tone of command in his voice was swoon-worthy, and she opened her mouth to give him what he wanted.

But the little red devil on her shoulder prompted her

to protest, "I'm not sure I should keep going. Some of my favorites are best left for...my own private enjoyment." She purred the words with wicked emphasis.

He whipped his head around, expression poleaxed. "You mean you've—" He stopped, grappling with how to phrase the question.

"Come while I was thinking about you?" she supplied helpfully. "Mmm-hmm."

They'd reached a building entrance, and he used his ID card again to unlock it. Right past the doors were elevators. The second they stepped inside one, his hands dropped to her hips and he hauled her against him for a crushing kiss that was both reward and punishment for all her teasing.

She thought she'd experienced heat in his arms before? Flames of pleasure consumed her. Arousal pulsed low in her body until she was slick with it, her breasts straining against the confines of her bra. The material was a satiny lace, but now it seemed almost scratchy, chafing her hypersensitive nipples. She didn't want silky fabric covering her; she wanted Daniel's broad palms and clever fingers.

The elevator doors parted with a ding, and she followed him blindly down a deserted hall, paying no attention to where they were or if she'd been in this building before. Despite her earlier nostalgia, the past no longer mattered. Neither did the future. All she cared about was the next hour and how quickly she could get Daniel out of his clothes.

He unlocked a door at the end of the hallway. Instead of flipping the light switch, he crossed the room, turning on a small lamp on the corner of the desk. He glanced down. "Good—the trash can is empty. The janitor's been here."

"Um…" He was worried about custodial efficiency at a time like this?

A slow smile spread across his face as he closed the office door and locked it. "That means no one will bother us."

"Oh." She beamed at him. Yay for empty trash cans.

He spread his hands in a welcoming gesture. "My office. Nothing fancy, but…"

"I like it." The small space held an eclectic assortment of books, a few framed pictures of him with important people—some she recognized, some she didn't—and best of all, a suede love seat below the window. She wasn't sure it was even technically big enough to qualify as a love seat, but it would work. Unless he preferred the desk. She ran her hand over a mug full of red pens. "This setting is enough to inspire a few role-playing fantasies."

He arched an eyebrow at her. "You mean like you were caught cheating and would do just about *anything* to convince me to let you stay in my class?"

"Hell, no." Even as a consensual pretense, men in authority positions exploiting young women was not a turn-on for her. "I mean like *I'm* the teacher. Who gives a slightly unorthodox final exam for her human sexuality class." She kicked off her shoes and reached for the clip holding up her French twist, letting her hair spill loose. "Think you can make the grade?"

He groaned. "I'm never going to be able to grade

papers in here again. How can I concentrate on soph-
omore essays when I'm rock hard and obsessed with
memories of you?"

"Sorry," she said without an ounce of contrition.
"I blame the little devil on my shoulder. She gives me
ideas."

Daniel curled his fingers in the soft knit of her
sweater and she obligingly raised her arms so he could
lift the garment over her head. "Honey, you don't have
a devil. More like a tour bus full of them who visit you
for creative inspiration on tormenting people."

"Is that what I do?" she asked, her breathing erratic
as he unbuttoned his shirt and revealed mouthwatering
abs. "Torment you?"

"In the best fucking ways." He lifted her to sit on
the edge of the desk and kissed her again. It wasn't
wildly out of control, like in the elevator, but this was
no less erotic. He took his time, teasing her, delving
into her mouth as his fingers ran up and down her bare
arms. As good as it felt, her triceps were not where she
needed to be touched. Squirming, she tried to lock her
legs around his waist, but he thwarted her with a half
step back.

She bit his bottom lip. "Talk about torment."

"Welcome to my world." There was a hint of laughter in his voice, but the amusement was strained with
desire.

"Keep it up, and you're going to get a failing grade."

He gave her an I-know-what-I'm-doing smile as he
straightened, reaching for his belt. "I promised you

we'd see each other naked. Now seems like the right time."

Her gaze was rapt as he unbuckled the belt and moved on to the fly of his slacks. Soon he was wearing only a pair of navy boxer briefs, the outline of his erection unmistakable.

She swallowed. "Don't stop now." It was supposed to be a demand; it sounded like a plea.

He hesitated, parroting her earlier coy tone. "I'm not sure I should keep going. After all, I'm down to just this." He dipped his thumb into the elastic waistband, inching the fabric past his hip bone.

Her eyes eagerly followed the trail of dark hair below his navel.

"But *you're* fully dressed except for one measly sweater." He gave her a pointed look. "Does that seem fair to you?"

She scrambled off the desk, shimmying out of her pants. It took her two attempts to unhook her bra, and she held Daniel's gaze as she let the lace flutter to the floor.

He ran a hand over his jaw, staring reverently. Her breasts were tight and full, swollen for his touch.

"Now we're even," she said, clad in nothing more than a pair of lacy bikini briefs. Her voice was raw with desire, nearly unrecognizable. If he didn't touch her soon, she would be forced to take matters into her own hands, dammit. She eased the lace down her legs, the satin a leisurely caress across her skin, and stepped out of the bottoms. Completely exposed, she raised an eyebrow to indicate it was his turn.

He was already reaching for her as he kicked free of his underwear. "You're beautiful." Closing what little space remained between them, he traced her collarbone with his thumbs before cupping her breasts.

She arched her back, offering herself up to him. Just as he'd threatened earlier, he started with slow, torturous circles that had her shifting weight from foot to foot before he *finally* rubbed across one nipple. A few strokes were enough to make her breath come in shallow pants, and he responded by tugging at the tip while he kissed the side of her neck, sucking with just enough pressure that there would probably be a faint mark. She was so wet now, so ready.

Craving more of him, she reached between their bodies, sliding her fingers down his shaft, loving the velvety texture. Softness stretched over unyielding hardness that was going to feel so damn good inside her. She gripped him tight, and he hissed out a breath between his teeth.

She relaxed her hand just long enough to do it again, and his hips jerked toward her. "Daniel, I was fantasizing about you in college. That's like ten years of foreplay. I want you now."

He nodded, his expression hungry. "Condom first." He turned in the direction of his discarded pants, but she moved faster, unzipping the purse she'd set on his desk.

"Here."

Taking it from her, he glanced at their options. "Sofa's probably more comfortable than the desk, fewer sharp edges." He caught her close, nuzzling her neck as his hand glided over the slope of her breast. "I've got all the sharp edges I can handle with you."

"Hey!"

"Perfect balance of sharp edges and lush curves." He followed his fingers with his mouth, licking a taut nipple, and the heat of his mouth blissed out all thought.

Her mind might have gone too blank to form words, but thankfully her legs were still steady enough to carry her to the love seat. He sat and she watched unabashedly as he smoothed the condom over his jutting cock. Resisting the urge to launch herself atop him, she teased them both by bending forward at the waist, loving his predatory gaze on the sway of her breasts, and framed his face in her hands, kissing him fiercely.

When she finally moved to straddle him, he stopped her with his hands at her hips. "Turn around?"

Curious, she did as requested. "Still looking for that second tattoo?" she joked breathlessly. It was small but too colorful to miss.

"No." He reached between her legs to stroke his thumb over the colorful image of tiny flowers amid a tangle of calligraphy vines. "Although I will want a closer look at it later." Without warning, he tugged her backward so that she tumbled onto his lap, facing away from him. It wasn't graceful, but it got her where she wanted to be—naked and on top of him.

He kissed the feather on her neck, running his tongue along it while his hands covered her breasts. She writhed, her soft cries escalating as he tweaked a nipple.

"You are drenched," he murmured at her ear as she ground against him. "I can feel you already."

She *was* drenched—and empty. Needy. With a whimper, she wiggled her hips, trying to find just the right angle, and he helped by pressing her forward with the flat of his hand against her spine. She raised up on the balls of her feet, and he positioned himself at her entrance, *right there*, the tip sliding into all that wetness, and she shuddered. He gripped her hips and thrust upward, spearing her with enough force that her body clenched around him, pleasure a bright starburst.

Her breath hitched, and she rotated forward, almost all the way off him, then slowly lowered herself until he was buried deep. He rolled his hips, rubbing against all the right places inside her, while his fingers were at her breast, tugging and pinching before soothing with softer touches. She babbled disjointed words of encouragement, like "yes" and "do that again" and *"Daniel."* With his free hand, he reached around her, grazing the narrow strip of hair between her legs before parting her folds and finding her clit. A groan reverberated through her and she rocked faster, giving herself over to a mindless rhythm that was all instinct and driving need and spiraling ecstasy.

So close. So good. So *much*. She was drowning in sensation and any minute that wave would come crashing down on her.

"God, Mia, you're…" His voice broke in a guttural noise as he clamped his fingers on her hips and he yanked her down on him. Her climax slammed through her, and she spasmed around him.

He bucked wildly. "Fuck, yes." He bit the juncture of her neck and shoulder, his cry muffled against her flesh as he came. Then he collapsed back against the couch, his strong arms around her midsection, holding her close.

Her heart thundered in her ears as she fought to catch her breath. That had been the kind of frenzied, pulse-pounding sex that incinerated one to a pile of satisfied ash. Eyes closed, she grinned inwardly. It was going to take a while for this phoenix to get feeling back in her legs, much less rise in a blaze of glory.

She turned her head to the side, resting it on his shoulder, loving the sensation of him surrounding her. The dark hair that dusted his chest was a not unpleasant rasp against her skin, and they were slick with each other's sweat. On impulse, she licked him, savoring the salty tartness.

"Mmm." He cradled her head in his hand, stroking her hair. "Honey, if you're going to start that up again, give me a minute to recover first."

Her muscles were limp with sensual satisfaction. If he could move at all, he had more stamina than she did. "Only a minute?"

"Maybe five. Half an hour, tops."

She laughed at that, but her amusement faded into a sigh. Half an hour from now, she should be at home. She needed to shower and fire up her laptop for one last review of the wedding details. "We can't start anything up again. I have to go."

"Same." His voice echoed her own wistful disappointment. "No offense to Eli, but I wish you were the one sleeping at my condo tonight."

"The problem," she said with a grin, "would be the lack of sleep. That was too good to only do once. A-plus work."

He gave her a very male smile, looking pleased with himself. "I always did test well." He traced the shell of her ear with his tongue, his voice a dark temptation. "Especially at oral exams."

She shivered but forced herself to move away from him. If she didn't, neither one of them would get any rest tonight.

"I don't want to leave," she said, trying to round up her discarded clothing. "But it's time."

"What if I refuse to take you home yet? We still have the desk…"

If only. "No distractions," she said sternly. Her grin probably ruined the reprimand. "I need to get to bed, and you are not invited." Not tonight, anyway. "I have to be up early to keep everything running smoothly tomorrow."

He rose, gathering his own clothes. "From what I saw today, you excel at it. I suppose that shouldn't be surprising. You always did like being in charge."

"Says the man who insisted on being the leader of every group project he was ever assigned."

"Guess we're both bossy." He kissed the top of her head, making it an endearment, not a complaint. Then he dropped more kisses below her ear, tracing his mouth along her jaw as he coaxed, "Ever give up control to someone else?"

"Not if I could help it." Delightfully wicked possibilities shuddered through her, all the things Daniel might do to her if she was under his power. *Like you aren't already halfway there?* "But there's a first time for everything, given the right motivation."

He scraped his teeth over her throat. "Challenge accepted."

She closed her eyes, melting into him for a moment before reality intruded. "Another time."

"Count on it."

KISSING MIA GOOD-NIGHT at her front door had been both sweetly intimate—more poignant now that they'd had sex—and achingly difficult. It was impossible to hold her, mouth locked on hers, absorbing her shuddery breaths and *mmm*s of encouragement, without wanting more. But, for the sake of his best friend and Mia's professional reputation, he'd told her to sleep well and managed to pull himself away.

He didn't trust himself not to turn around and go back until he made it all the way to his condo's parking garage. Skipping the elevator, he subjected himself to flights of stairs to burn away the restless energy that had built during his drive while he mentally replayed their evening. Sex with Mia had been phenomenal; he should be sated, bonelessly content. Yet recalling each erotic detail left him hard and wanting again. He clung to the addictive draw of her kisses, the sweet weight of her breasts in his hands, the gloriously uncivilized sound of their bodies slapping together as they'd rocked toward orgasm.

Oh, hell. He'd reached his hallway and was even more turned on than when he'd parked the car. *Think about something else!* Unlocking his door, he cast about for possibilities, trying to occupy his mind. Baseball stats, an alphabetical listing of characters in *King Lear*, the tedious prospect of a fund-raiser he'd promised his family he'd attend next month.

"Hey." Eli looked up from the couch when the door opened. A tumbler of bourbon sat on the marble-topped coffee table in front of him, and he had his phone in his hand. "I was just texting Bex sweet dreams. And trying to remember why the hell we decided to spend the night apart," he grumbled. "There's no one else I'd rather be with right now. No offense."

Daniel chuckled. "None taken. Believe me." He crossed the room to the minibar and poured himself a bourbon. "Been here long?"

"Just got here. Dad and I went for coffee—decaf, not that I'll be able to sleep a wink tonight either way. He had some fatherly wisdom to impart. It took him an hour and a half but boiled down to, don't piss her off, but, since you will anyway, don't be too stubborn to apologize."

"Seems to me you've already got that mastered. Meant to thank you for the suggestion of flowers, by the way." He wasn't sure how much the bouquet itself had thawed Mia's attitude toward him, but checking to see if she'd received it had provided an excuse to call and win her over. "She forgave me."

"Yeah. I noticed that you and the fine wedding coordinator were pretty cozy tonight. You might actually have a chance with her."

Daniel grinned into his drink, too refined to kiss and tell.

But apparently he had no semblance of a poker face, because Eli let out a startled laugh. "You're *kidding*. Nice going, man. Mia's the total package—savvy, sassy, sexy. Almost in the same league as my Bex." He held up his glass in an across-the-room toast. "Damn, we have good taste in women."

"I'll drink to that."

They chatted for a few minutes about plans for tomorrow, but Eli's cell phone kept chiming. Texts from acquaintances who couldn't make the ceremony but wanted to send congratulations, a question from a relative about the reception menu, a tipsy prank call from the bride-to-be. When that one came in, Eli excused himself for the night, retiring to his room with a grin.

Daniel heard muffled laughter through the wall as he rinsed out his glass in the kitchen. Would it seem too needy if he called Mia after already telling her good-night?

He headed to his room and took a quick shower, but the impulse to talk to her didn't subside. She was probably either busy with last-minute preparations or getting ready to turn in, but he wanted to hear her voice almost as much as he wished he was kissing her right now. He climbed into bed, the room dark except for the soft lamp he'd planned to read by. Instead of reaching for the seven-hundred-page fantasy novel on his nightstand, he grabbed his cell phone.

His compromise with himself was that, rather than calling, he'd send her a quick text that could be ignored if she was working or asleep. He started to type a message about how much tonight had meant to him but deleted it immediately, deciding to send something silly that would amuse Mia and her shoulder devil.

I know you already gave me an A plus, but I'm a perfectionist. I'd love to discuss the possibility of extra credit sometime.

A second later, her response illuminated the screen. Don't you mean sextra credit?

He laughed even as he rolled his eyes. Terrible puns are below your dignity.

Nah, dignity is overrated. Great sex is never dignified. It's a little noisy, a little messy and a LOT of fun. Three dots appeared, followed by, You'd better be taking notes. There will be a quiz.

Her playfully bossy tone was so clear in his head, it was almost as if she was in the room with him. He turned off the lamp, wanting the only light to be from the phone, from their flirting, shutting out the rest of the world. What if I have questions about the material? he typed. Can I come to you for private tutoring?

You can come to me. Or in me. Or on me.

Lust surged through him and he gripped his phone so hard it was a wonder the screen didn't crack. He was breathing hard, the mental images her words conjured filthy hot. He hadn't yet decided on a response when her next message came through.

Did I shock you?

Shocked, no. Aroused to the brink of pain, yes.

Poor baby. If I was there I could kiss it and make it better.

Daniel groaned softly at the thought of her mouth on him. Mia had edge. He recalled her almost deliciously cruel grip when she'd squeezed his dick in her soft hand. Her version of kissing it all better might involve teeth. But however she did it, he knew it would be good. *The best.* He resolved to be that for her, too. In retrospect, he wished he'd gone slower tonight. She'd told him she was ready, and there was no question that she'd climaxed hard. Her cries still rang in his ears, and when she came, she'd tightened around him in rhythmic clenches that had propelled him to his own release. So, yeah, the sex had been great. But what if he'd taken the time to drive her even wilder? To stoke the fire so hot that even her friendly devil was calling for ice water and mercy?

I'm not sure I lived up to my full potential tonight.

She sent him a wide-eyed emoji. Don't know whether to be intrigued or alarmed. Any more "potential" and I'd be walking funny.

Tomorrow would be an interesting challenge. If he grew hard every time he looked at her, he'd be walking pretty damn funny by the end of the day himself.

More words popped up on his screen. Pop quiz! If you had it to do over again, to demonstrate your full potential, what would you do differently?

That was easy. He'd already considered it on the car ride home, thinking about the next time they had sex. *Soon*, he hoped. Tonight, he'd spun her facing away from him. He'd wanted to see that absurdly sexy feather tattoo when he pumped inside her.

The position had made it easy to touch all her most sensitive places, but only with his hands. Now that he'd experienced how responsive she was, how turned on she got when he played with her breasts, he wished he'd been better able to explore them with his mouth. So he gave her the raw, uncensored truth, remembering how her eyes had darkened at the restaurant when he talked dirty to her. I'd spend more time tonguing your gorgeous tits. Discovering what makes you wetter—slow licks or the graze of my teeth or sucking you until you couldn't take it anymore.

Three dots appeared, then vanished and reappeared again. He waited expectantly, needing to know how his words had affected her, but no text appeared. Instead, his phone rang.

Excitement pulsed through him as he answered. "Hello?"

"Daniel." The sound of his name from her lips reminded him of how she'd chanted it while she rode him. "Now that we're *both* aroused to the point of pain, what are we going to do about it?"

7

IN A NIGHT full of steamy surprises and blistering pleasure, perhaps the biggest revelation was that Daniel Keegan was capable of sexting. After he'd dropped her off, Mia had tried her best to work but her focus was shot. She'd been shutting down the laptop and was considering calling him when his first message had appeared on her phone, asking about extra credit. She'd been amused.

But she wasn't amused anymore. She was so turned on she was trembling. Her last attempt at a text had been a typo-riddled mess, so she'd called instead. Besides, she wanted to hear that low voice, wanted to close her eyes and feel it slide over her.

"I don't suppose my driving across town and carrying you to bed is an option?" he asked.

She bit back a moan at how good that idea sounded.

"Or are you in bed already?" His tone was a mix of curiosity and ragged desire. As if he was picturing her there. As if he was picturing himself with her.

She shook her head before realizing he couldn't see. "Living room. I'm stretched across the couch." It was buttery smooth leather, a very comfortable piece of furniture; she'd never once regretted the pricy splurge. But had she stayed on the couch instead of working in her room because it was so comfy…or because it made her think of the little sofa in Daniel's office? Of the way he'd pulled her across his lap, stroking into her at the perfect angle? "If only you were here with me."

"I can be out the door in three minutes."

She sighed. "Bad idea. At least, that's what the rational half of my brain says." The devil on her shoulder whispered *Invite him over and greet him naked at the door.* Easy for the devil to say—*she* didn't have to pay rent with the money from this wedding and resulting referrals. "Maybe I should just take a cold shower."

"You, naked under a spray of water?" He groaned. "You're killing me."

Then it would be mutual murder. Her voice felt thick in her throat, probably because she was choking on lust. "Don't you like picturing me naked?"

"Hell, yes. But I like picturing you in clothes, too, so I can imagine undressing you myself, baring you, getting us both hot."

His words drizzled over her, rich and sweet like syrup. Which she would no doubt ask him to lick off of her.

"Besides," he added, "when you're dressed, I get to imagine what you're wearing—or not wearing—beneath your clothes. The sheer lace bra and panties you had on tonight will haunt my dreams."

She grinned, reminding herself how lucky she was to have a friend who got her a steep discount on extravagant lingerie, and started mentally reviewing her options for tomorrow.

"How trite would it be to ask, what are you wearing?"

"Don't think of it as trite, Professor. Think of it as quoting a classic."

"Classic, huh?" He chuckled softly. "Chaucer, Poe, Dante…and lots of horny teenage boys before caller ID was invented."

"For the record, I'm wearing a ratty T-shirt I won playing trivia in a bar. But I've got on a pair of scarlet string-bikini panties, so I'm not a complete loss."

"Brains plus sex appeal. You are the total package."

"Flatterer." Wicked inspiration struck. She hit the speakerphone button so she could still talk to him as she used both hands to slide her panties down. Then she set them on a sofa cushion and snapped a picture of the bright red fabric against the leather. "I'm texting you something. So you'll have a better visual of my wardrobe."

"Let me guess," he said with wry humor. "A close-up of a bar logo on your sh—" He broke off with a sharp intake of breath.

"They're pretty, right? I have quite a collection."

"If you're not wearing those anymore…"

"I'm naked from the waist down."

He snarled in frustration. "If I'd got in my car when you first called, I could be there by now." Only if he ignored pretty much every traffic law in existence, but she appreciated the sentiment. "Then your shirt would be history, too. I wish I was there to rip it off."

"I could do it for you." Anything to deepen that rough desire she craved in his tone.

There was a pause. Maybe she'd surprised him with the offer. Or maybe he was just savoring the mental image.

"Do it," he rasped. "Put the shirt with the panties. Send me another picture."

So that he would know she was truly naked. The idea made her shiver. Why did standing in her own apartment, alone and unclothed, seem intimately revealing? No one but Daniel would ever know, and he'd already seen all of her. Still, something like nervous excitement pulsed in her belly. She grabbed the frayed hem of the soft-from-a-thousand-washings T and pulled it over her head with a whisper of cotton. "Done."

Superficially, the photo was innocent enough to be downright boring. Just a faded shirt tossed on the sofa, bright red fabric peeking out from beneath it. Yet she got an erotic thrill when she hit Send.

"Good girl," he said hoarsely.

"Good? I've heard the opposite a time or two."

"But you'll be good for me, won't you, honey?" His voice was low and coaxing, full of dark persuasion that made her weak in the knees. "Do me one little favor?"

She sank back to the couch. Her throat had gone dry, and she reached for the glass of water on the end table before answering, "What favor might that be?" She had some guesses.

"Since I couldn't be there to remove your T-shirt, you took care of it for me. And since I'm not there to touch you..."

Anticipation buzzed through her. He wanted her to touch herself while he listened on the other end. Professor "Humdrum" Keegan had a seriously naughty side.

"Mia?" he prompted.

"Yes." She would definitely oblige him. As excruciatingly turned on as she was, there'd been no way she was going to sleep tonight without masturbating. She reclined across the couch, scooting down so that her knees were draped over the arm, legs dangling and pelvis tipped upward. The cool leather felt good against her bare skin, but not as good as Daniel moving over her would have been.

"What would you do?" she whispered. "If you were here."

"First, I'd kiss you."

"Afraid I can't help you with that."

"Close your eyes. Run a finger over your lips, slowly. A kiss hello."

She did exactly as he asked, sighing against the pad of her middle finger.

"Our kiss wouldn't stay tender for long. I'd want inside your delectable mouth, would want to feel your tongue against mine. Lick your finger for me."

Shuddering at the command in his tone, she followed his instructions with enthusiasm, sucking at her own finger as if he could see her performance, running her tongue up the side and across the tip.

"Is it nice and wet?"

She didn't think he really meant her finger. *"Yes."* Neither did she.

"Rub your nipple, then the other one. They're hard aren't they?"

She didn't even try to talk this time, just moaned at the sensation of her fingers strumming the taut peaks and Daniel's sexy words in her ear.

"I'm hard for you, too," he murmured, a catch in his voice that told her she wasn't the only one touching herself.

She was almost jealous as she imagined those blunt male fingers circling his erection; she selfishly wanted to be the one wringing pleasure from him. "I've changed my mind. Get in your car and get over here."

His laugh had a desperate edge. "Too late for that. Run your hands up the inside of your thighs. When I touched the tattoo there earlier, you shook. Because you're ticklish, or because you couldn't wait for me to reach your pussy?"

"Both."

"I've reached it now," he told her. "Parting the plump lips, fingering your clit."

As she matched her actions to his words, she realized how long it had been since she'd touched herself this way. She normally used her vibrator, which was very effective, but not as personal. Increasing tempo and friction, she groaned, and Daniel echoed it.

"I want…" His words sounded as if they came through gritted teeth, as if he were fighting off his own release until she found hers. She wished he would let go. Hearing his loss of control, imagining him coming in hot waves, would probably send her over the edge. "Want to be inside you. So fucking badly."

She slid a finger inside herself. "You are." In her fantasy, in their shared fantasy, he was driving into her. She added a second finger, arching her back. Her breath was choppy, her left leg had slid off the couch, leaving her wantonly spread and open. With her other hand, she rubbed madly at her clit, sensation a tight promise at the base of her spine, the explosion building. Imminent.

"*Mia.*" It was a muted roar, with the intensity of a shout if not the volume.

Answering him with a wordless cry, she clenched around her fingers as the orgasm broke over her. Her heart was racing so hard he could probably hear it over the phone.

"Christ," he muttered. "That…"

She nodded, unable to find her voice. For long minutes, their only conversation was panting breaths and contented silence.

Finally, he asked, "Better?"

"Much," she said with a happy sigh. "Before, I was too keyed up to sleep. Now I'll be out like a light."

"You may be on to something. I've had insomnia for a few weeks. Maybe this will help."

"I hope so. You're my unofficial date to the wedding." Obviously, she would be there in a professional capacity and had plenty to keep her busy. But she planned on taking him home with her tomorrow night when it was all over. "For the kind of after-party I have in mind, you'd better be well rested."

MIA STOOD AT the back of the beautifully decorated room, uncharacteristically misty as Eli and Bex exchanged their vows. The bride was stunning in a dress that started with a beaded white bodice, then cascaded into a red-and-gold ankara skirt. Eli wore a suit, his tie custom-made to match the print on the wedding gown. They were a gorgeous, striking couple.

Yet Mia's gaze kept straying toward the best man who stood with them. Daniel carried off his suit splendidly, but she wasn't mesmerized by him just because he was so damn easy on the eyes. She was transfixed by the memories of the night before, the amazing connection they'd shared. First times with a new lover could be awkward. But sex with Daniel had been breathtaking. *And to think, I once called him unimaginative.* She'd never been so utterly grateful to be wrong.

A cheer went up from the guests as Eli kissed his new wife, and Mia breathed her customary sigh of relief. The ceremony had gone off without a hitch. The closest they'd come to last-minute crises were that the officiant had been ten minutes late and the father of the bride had lost a button off his suit. Mia was able to fix that; she had a key to a small room at the back of the complex that held mismatched pieces of furniture, paper products and emergency supplies, like first aid provisions, flashlights and a sewing kit. She liked to think that if any larger problems had cropped up, she would have handled them with efficient grace, but she was happy not to test that theory when she was so distracted by Daniel. There was still the reception to follow, but in her experience, clients and their families remained calmer about any mishaps that took place once the solemn part was over. The champagne probably helped.

With the wedding concluded, it was her job to direct guests into the connected building where the reception was being held. She would serve as unofficial hostess while the wedding party and the newlyweds' families stayed behind for pictures at the altar. She was almost too busy to dwell on her date as she answered questions about where the bathrooms were located, handed her business card to a few people and oversaw distribution of the appetizers. When Bex caught up to her half an hour later, the food was one of the things she praised Mia for.

The beaming bride crushed her in a quick hug. "Thank you *so* much. For everything."

"My pleasure," Mia said sincerely. But then she flashed a teasing grin. "Especially with what I'm charging you."

Bex laughed. "You've been a godsend. Even if all you did was wrangle my parents, your fee would have been worth it. And I know I didn't think it would be necessary, coming from a family of serious carnivores, but bless you for persuading me to add a vegan entrée to the menu. Turns out, my boss's wife is a vegetarian and my cousin's date has a dairy allergy, so vegan takes care of that. There are probably others, too."

"I'm glad you're happy with everything." Mia lowered her voice to a confidential tone. "And, in a way, you and Eli did me a favor. Because of you guys, I crossed paths with Daniel again."

"I hope that later, after dinner's served and everything settles down, you two will find time for a dance. Or something," she added slyly.

Heat rose in Mia's cheeks, startling her. She was not a woman who blushed. At least, not usually. But she couldn't help vividly recalling just how good Daniel was at "or something."

Bex patted her arm. "It's funny how things work out. I was so sad for him when Felicity turned down his proposal, but now I—"

"Proposal?" She'd known he recently went through a breakup; she'd had no idea he'd proposed marriage. The relationship must have been very serious.

"Oh." Bex rocked back, her expression stricken. "You didn't know?"

"It's not a big deal," Mia hastened to assure her. Rule number one was keeping the bride happy. "He told me it was a long-term relationship, I was just fuzzy on the details. We honestly haven't talked much about her."

"Because you've helped him get over her."

Smiling politely, Mia bit back her automatic protest. She and Daniel had only spent a week exploring their attraction. Phone sex and a single encounter in his office were not significant signs that he'd moved on from a relationship that had spanned years of his life. They were more likely indicators of a rebound fling.

"Is this a ladies-only chat?" Eli asked, looping his arms around his wife's waist from behind. "Or can anyone join? I know it's only been a few minutes, but I missed you."

Bex craned her head, stretching up on her toes to

meet him for a quick kiss. "Was I neglecting you, boo? Sorry. You make me so happy, I just want to see everyone else happy, too. I was telling Mia that she's good for Daniel."

Eli shot Mia an earnest look over his bride's head. "He really likes you, in case he didn't make that clear."

"Oh, he did." That ridiculous stinging warmth was back in her face, and she ducked her gaze.

"He's one of the best men I know," Eli added. "No wedding pun intended. He comes across as a little formal, at times." Obviously he was too loyal to say "stuffy" or "uptight." "But once you get to know him—"

"I've already realized there's more to him than a starchy first impression. He's...multifaceted." She doubted Daniel's friend knew just how much. "But today is about you two! Go mingle with your guests and soak up the well wishes."

Bex laughed at her bossy tone. "Guess we better listen to her," she told Eli. "We did put her in charge."

They disappeared back into the happy crowd, which did not—as far as Mia could tell—include Daniel. Also missing were the two ushers. She suspected the three of them were out decorating Eli's car before it got dark. Then, suddenly, a finger traced over the tattoo on her neck, unerringly finding it beneath the thick curls she'd left loose to soften the severity of her red suit.

Her happiness to see him as she turned was nearly electric. "Hi." Their gazes collided. *I'd kiss you but I'm on duty.*

He brushed his thumb over her bottom lip for the barest second before dropping his hand to his side. *I know.* "Hi, yourself. If I didn't mention it earlier, you look fantastic."

Her smile spread. "You did." They'd only seen each other for a few minutes before the ceremony, and they'd been surrounded by other people. He'd sounded so proper when he'd told her she looked lovely. There was nothing proper about the heat in his eyes now.

"Classy suit." His gaze lingered on the jacket. "Very…buttoned up." His right hand curled into a loose fist, as if he were battling the urge to reach for the buttons.

She sighed over his words from the night before, that the fun of her being in clothes was the chance to take them off of her. *Baring you, getting us both hot.* Damn it, she'd had fragments of that phone call echoing in her head all day, arousal simmering like a low-grade fever while she tried to get her job done. Try as she might, it was impossible to shake the memory. Why couldn't she just get some Taylor Swift song stuck in her head like everyone else?

"Uh-oh." He noticed her scowl. "Everything all right?"

"Yes. But we should start seating for dinner in a moment. Ready to give your best man toast?"

He nodded. "I just hope I don't yawn my way through it."

"Insomnia still?" She'd slept like the dead until her alarm blared at her this morning. "Even after our… conversation?"

"Oh, I fell asleep with no trouble at all. But I woke up again at four in the morning. It worked out okay, though. Eli was too excited to sleep and when I heard him moving around, I suggested we go to the Hash Brown Hut like we used to back in the day."

She wrinkled her nose at the mention of the twenty-four-hour diner, known for their breakfast-only menu and food so greasy that even the air was slimy with it. She'd only been once, with some drunk friends in college during finals week; she'd still had the indigestion to remember them by when they went home for the summer. "What kind of best man takes the groom to get food poisoning on the morning of his wedding?"

"You don't like the Hut?" He gave her a chiding look. "It's an Atlanta landmark."

"So is the Center for Disease Control, but I don't go there to eat, either."

He guffawed at that.

"Ms. Hayes?" One of the catering staff approached, an apprehensive expression on his face. "There's a slight situation with the desserts."

She frowned. "How slight?" With a hand on his shoulder to lead him to the side—one did not discuss potential problems in front of the guests—she flashed Daniel a contrite smile.

He gave an understanding nod and merged back into the throng, leaving her to do her job. The next hour passed quickly as she dealt with dessert issues, made some last-minute seating adjustments before dinner was served and conferred with the DJ about the chosen songs for the couple's first dance and the father-daughter dance that would make everyone cry; she also chatted with him about an upcoming event she wanted to contract him for.

She was standing at the back of the candlelit room, surveying to make sure no one needed anything, when Daniel rose to give his toast. For all that he claimed not to enjoy crowded social situations, he seemed perfectly at ease speaking in front of everyone. She supposed teaching helped with that. He took the time-honored approach of opening with a joke, one that was safely acceptable—even for a Keegan—but funny enough to draw legitimate laughter. After that, his words quickly turned heartfelt; it was clear Bex and Eli meant a lot to him. But as he discussed the sacred importance of marriage, of finding the right partner to share one's life with, Mia's stomach knotted.

On their first date, he'd told her he'd just been through a breakup. *With a woman I'd been seeing on-and-off since middle school.* He'd said it casually, but marriage was a permanent proposition, not one he would take lightly. Mia couldn't help wondering about the unseen woman who'd meant enough to him that he'd proposed. Was it possible he still loved her?

Daniel was a highly principled man. Mia wasn't sure he'd be able to do all of the things—*say* all of the things—he had to her if his heart belonged to someone else. Still, that didn't mean he was over Felicity. Maybe that's what his affair with Mia and his wildly uncharacteristic behavior were about; she'd seen Wren and Shannon act out after breakups, redefining or re-claiming their identity outside of couplehood. Hell, she'd been through it herself, although Mia had been so focused on establishing her company, it had been a while since she'd had a real relationship.

Just don't get any crazy ideas about this *being one.*

She and Daniel generated sparks, and she didn't want to give that up too soon. But in the long run? They'd drive each other insane. Years from now, he would marry someone more suitable. Mia could just imagine their country club reception.

After toasts from the maid of honor and both fathers, it was time to cut the cake. Mia had been to weddings where the bride and groom thought it was funny to mash cake into each other's faces, but either Bex and Eli were too classy for that or they were just in a hurry to get to the dancing. They'd taken swing lessons last fall especially for their introductory dance; Bex admitted it hadn't been easy to juggle the classes with her schedule at the hospital but, "That's the point, right? If you love someone, you make the time." That philosophy would serve the Wallaces well in their new life together.

The couple's first dance was as showstopping as they could have hoped for; given Eli's notable height and strength, he was able to pick Bex up and toss her around as if she barely weighed a thing. What woman wouldn't enjoy that? Soon, other guests had kicked off their shoes and taken to the floor. Daniel hung back. He'd left his jacket on his chair, but looked otherwise freshly pressed in his suit and tie. Mia felt the now familiar compulsion to disrupt all that crisp perfection. She wanted to see him with his hair mussed, his shirt creased from holding her tight against him.

She was so taken by the mental image that when he walked up to her, it was all she could do not to immediately tousle his hair into disarray.

"Full disclosure," he said grimly, "I don't enjoy dancing. I'm good at it, technically. Cotillion was a required part of my adolescence."

"Ugh. No wonder you don't enjoy it. Remind me to take you to a club some night with a deep, throbbing bass you can feel through the floor and dim lighting that encourages illicit acts." She grabbed his tie and tugged him closer. "I'll show you what real dancing is like."

"Does it have to be a club?" His voice lowered. "Maybe you could give me lessons at my apartment."

"And would we be naked during these lessons?" she asked laughingly.

"I…" His eyes were glazed with desire. "What were we talking about? I heard 'naked' and everything else is a meaningless buzz."

"You were telling me you don't like to dance."

"Right." He glanced toward the enthusiastic participants out on the floor. "But if you want to, I—"

"Ms. Hayes?"

Mia turned, her eyes narrowing as she identified the speaker. "You." It was Eli's cousin Terrence, who'd told her at the bachelor party that he thought she was even prettier than the dancers on stage—but that he'd need to see her undressed to judge for sure. He'd also suggested, with a lewd gesture at his crotch, that if her skimpy outfit wasn't keeping her warm enough, he had just the thing to heat up her night. It was good

Daniel had come along and dragged Terrence bodily from the party, or she might have resorted to violence.

Now, Daniel put his arm around her shoulder, pulling her snugly against him as he stared the man down.

Terrence shrank back from their united front, nervously glancing from the two of them over his shoulder toward Eli's mother. It was a wonder Shirley Wallace's laser-focused glare wasn't burning holes through her nephew's suit; frankly, setting his orange-and-magenta tie on fire would be a mercy. "I, ah, had too much to drink at Eli's stag party. Forgot my manners," he muttered. "Auntie Shirl thought maybe it would be a good idea for me to come apologize."

Mia couldn't help rolling her eyes. "You couldn't figure that out on your own? You're a grown man. No one should have to send you over to say you're sorry like a reluctant fourth grader."

"Hey, I—" Whatever he saw in Daniel's expression shut him up.

"If you 'forget your manners' when you drink," she added, "maybe ease up on the alcohol." She wondered absently if she should talk to the bartender about watering down Terrence's cocktails.

"Yeah. Yeah, I could do that."

"Then I accept your apology, but only if you promise not to treat other women like that, either."

"If you do," Daniel said mildly, "and Eli hears of it, we might have to come give you a refresher on manners."

Terrence tugged at the buttoned collar of his shirt. "Not necessary, man. One-time-only mistake. Isolated incident." He flashed Mia a pained smile, then informed his aunt, from a safe distance, "We're all good here, Shirl." Then he scuttled to the opposite side of the room.

"He seemed genuinely scared of you," Mia said. "Just how many times did he 'bump his head' getting into that cab?"

Daniel bared his teeth in a shark's smile. "He shouldn't have touched you." The words were matter-of-fact, but the gleam of possessiveness in his silvery eyes was so primal it made her shiver.

She glanced around the room, watching caterers collect empty dishes and smiling guests unwind on the dance floor and in chatty clusters by the bar. No one would miss Mia for a few minutes. "Come with me," she said, as out of breath as if she'd been swing-dancing alongside the bride and groom.

They rounded a corner into a back hallway, uncannily quiet after the music and noise of the reception. From the pocket of her suit jacket, she pulled out a key to the small room that had once been an administrator's office. Now it was just spare storage. They stepped inside, and she closed the door behind them. He backed her into the wall, letting the anticipation build before he lowered his head and captured her lips. She grinned into his mouth, thinking that he tasted like buttercream frosting and sin.

Pulling back long enough to study her expression, he asked, "What's so funny?"

"Nothing. But remind me to write a letter to ice

cream companies and tell them I have an idea for a great new flavor."

One eyebrow rose in an endearingly confused expression that crinkled his forehead. "Not sure I understand how your mind works."

"Probably because I'm a little offbeat," she admitted. She let her head fall back against the wall as he kissed her neck. "But you proved last night you definitely understand how my body works."

His lips curled in the barest hint of a cocky grin as he reached for the top button of her jacket.

Should she stop him? *But this is exactly why you chose this outfit.* For Daniel. She decided to let him have this moment—she wanted to see his reaction too badly to deny either of them. It would only take her a minute to rebutton.

She looked every inch the professional in her suit skirt and red jacket, a bit of prim white blouse showing through. It wasn't until Daniel reached the second button that he realized just how see-through the blouse was, prominently displaying the black lace bra under it. Groaning, eyes locked on her chest, he fumbled with the remaining buttons.

"It comes with matching panties." She stood on her tiptoes, catching his earlobe between her teeth. "And thigh-highs."

"Show me."

Sweet heaven, that voice. It made her want to do unspeakable things. Made her want to do anything he asked. She hesitated, not to be coy but because she didn't entirely trust herself. As appealing as the idea of a disheveled Daniel was, she didn't want to walk back into that reception looking completely debauched.

"We can't have sex," she said firmly. "Not until we get back to my place."

"But I can kiss you." It wasn't a question. His mouth was already on hers again, the thrust of his tongue making her body hum. "And I want to see you," he said several heated moments later.

With a palm flat on his chest, she gently pushed him away to give her room to move. He'd left no space between them, crowding her in the most spectacular way, filling her senses. After he obligingly backed up, she shrugged out of her jacket, and folded it neatly over the back of an upholstered antique chair. Next, the blouse. Finally, she reached behind her waist to unzip the skirt, shimmying out of it with a pronounced wiggle for Daniel's benefit.

Once she'd finished stripping, she was left with a black demi-bra, tanga panties, silk thigh-highs and a pair of peep-toe pumps.

He swallowed hard.

"Courtesy of my friend Wren," she said, stretching her arms over her head to give him an unimpeded view. "She's the manager of a very nice lingerie store."

"I owe Wren a drink. Or possibly a tropical vacation." He advanced on her, the possessive light in his gaze even brighter than before. That expression said she was his and that he was biding his time deciding where to touch her first, deciding how to make her shudder and clutch at him and lose her mind.

"This is only a preview for later," she said, starting

to get nervous. With that look in his eyes, it wouldn't take him long to shred her self-control or her common sense. "No sex, remember?"

"I wouldn't dream of it." He gave her a look of such patently false innocence that her heart skipped a beat. Whatever devil Daniel had on *his* shoulder was running the show now. "But I want to give you a preview of what's to come, too." Bracing her against the wall with a hand on her hip, he sank to his knees.

The sight of his dark head as he kissed along the lace-topped edge of her thigh-high was unbearably suggestive. Having him between her legs made her throb with the need to feel his mouth higher up. He teased his tongue over her tattoo, stopping to really study it.

"Is this…your name?" He sounded as if he didn't know whether to be incredulous or amused.

"Yeah." It wasn't immediately obvious, but the green vines surrounding the flowers were curlicues that spelled out Mia. "I know most people get someone else's name inked on them."

He glanced up with a smile, and she tried not to hyperventilate at how hot he looked kneeling in front of her. "You're not most people," he said, earning a grin that melted into a sigh when he traced his finger over the artwork, the light touch trembling along her nerve endings. "So why'd you choose this?"

"It was a reminder that I answer to myself. I don't have to share my body with anyone unless I want to and I don't have to justify my choices or my clothes or my curves to anyone else."

He frowned, looking as if he were about to question her further.

Her hands dropped to his shoulders, lightly shoving. "We should get back."

"We will. But you did say I could kiss you."

Her eyes slid shut as his mouth slid up the sensitive skin. Higher and higher until—

"Mia." His voice was awestruck.

She grinned, knowing he'd just realized there was a slit in the black lace. The crotchless panties were supposed to have been a surprise for later. "You like?"

He answered her with his eyes, gaze locked on hers as he used both hands to widen the opening in the fabric, letting his fingertips brush over her in a tantalizing prelude. Then he was spreading *her* open, and molten need rushed through her as he leaned in to flick his tongue over her clit. She gasped, her fingers digging into his shoulders. Another very precise swipe of his tongue, and her world tilted. Then another, accompanied by a low growl in his throat as he sucked. She bucked toward the wet heat of his mouth, wanting to lose herself in it, wondering if this was how he felt when he was inside her.

Her response seemed to set him off. He licked faster, lashing her with pleasure, as he slipped a finger inside her. The sensations were overpowering. If she hadn't been pinned to the wall, she wouldn't have been able to stay on her feet. Even with the support at her back, she'd blindly reached out one hand to grip the nearby shelving unit. Her other hand was tangled in his hair, tightening reflexively as he scraped his teeth against her.

The tiny sting magnified everything she was feeling, bringing the spinning intensity into sharper focus, and she relinquished her hold on the back of his head to press her hand against her mouth, doing her damnedest not to scream. Pumping his fingers in and out of her, he used his teeth again, and flames shot through her blood. Her body couldn't contain it.

One more of those wickedly sharp caresses, and she was going to go supernova. She whimpered, afraid she was about to yell his name so loudly she'd be heard in Alabama. He crooked a finger inside her as he sucked, and shock waves of bliss rocked through her, unending pulses that buckled her knees. He lapped at her as she came, groaning as if he couldn't get enough of her, not stopping until she slumped forward.

He caught her against his chest and eased her to the floor with him. "I got you," he murmured, smoothing a hand over her hair.

She angled her head, blindly seeking a kiss, tasting herself on his tongue and trying to burrow even closer, knowing she wouldn't be satisfied until her naked limbs were tangled with his, so intertwined that it would be difficult to tell where one of them stopped and the other started.

"Congratulations," she said, her voice scratchy from the cries she'd done her best to muffle. "You're officially in charge of locking up when this shindig is over. I don't think I'll be able to stand. The storage room is my home now. Forward my mail."

He chuckled affectionately. "Careful. With the

slurred speech and nonsense talk, people will think you've been hitting the champagne."

"I ought to hit *you*." She balled up one fist and raised it about two inches before letting it fall limply to her side. "I can't believe you did that to me when I still have work to do. Be a dear and pretend I socked you in the shoulder."

"Oh, the pain," he said in a dry monotone. "Ow. The agony."

She laughed out loud. "Ever the obliging gentleman."

He stood, helping her to her feet. "I try." He passed her the skirt and blouse, but when it came time for the jacket, he swatted her hand away, wanting to be the one to rebutton it.

"Do I look okay?" she asked, finger-combing her hair and hoping for the best.

His gaze slid slowly over her body, and by the time it returned to her face, that suggestive gleam was back.

She scrambled for the doorknob. "Forget I asked."

Chuckling, he took her hand, and they strolled down the hall, parting ways just outside the reception.

"The caterers should be packing up," Mia said with a glance at her watch. "I want to check in with them one last time."

He nodded, giving her fingers a quick squeeze. "Go be professional. I'll see you later. Oh and, Mia?" he added when she'd taken a few steps away. "I don't know what new ice cream flavor you're planning to recommend, but I can sure as hell tell you what *my* new favorite flavor is."

"UM. WOW?"

Straightening from the lamp he'd just turned on, Daniel turned toward Mia. She was getting her first look at his place, but despite the wow, she didn't seem impressed. More apprehensive, judging from her frown and slumped shoulders. Although, her posture could just be fatigue.

They'd decided to go back to his condo since it was after midnight and he lived closer. They could pick up her car tomorrow. She'd told him he could leave the solarium without her and she'd meet him later, but he'd waited. He had wanted to help. Or at least—if she preferred he stay out of the way—watch her in motion. Pathetic, his friend Sean would say, that he was so fascinated with a woman that he enjoyed being near enough just to hear her tell someone else where to store stacked chairs.

Standing in the center of his living room, Mia turned a slow circle, taking in everything from the floor-to-ceiling window to the white carpet that was so thick it silenced footsteps to the five-by-five piece of original art hanging over the fireplace he'd never used. Finally, she said, "You are never invited to my apartment."

"What?" Not the assessment he'd expected. "Why not?"

"Because, compared to you, I live in a slum. Look at this view!" She gestured toward the brightly lit Atlanta skyline. "My place overlooks the Dumpster behind a liquor store. And that painting? Hardly a garage sale find."

"It was a Christmas gift from my parents a couple of years ago." Realizing how much it had probably cost, he changed the subject. "Can I get you anything?" he asked as he dropped his jacket and tie in a chair. "A nightcap? A cup of coffee? Glass of water?"

"Like tap water, or a fifty-dollar bottle that comes from a fairy-guarded spring in Patagonia?"

"It's forty-five dollars a bottle, and they're not technically fairies, they're water sprites." He was glad to see her face light up when she smiled. Was she really intimidated by his place? College professors weren't rich, although he had a Keegan inheritance from his grandparents that had performed reasonably well in the stock market.

"Water would be great," she said, sounding more like herself. She walked over to the sofa and kicked off her shoes with a small, blissful moan, flexing her newly freed toes.

"So was today typical for you?" he asked. He was exhausted, and he hadn't even arrived at the solarium as early as she had. Nor had he endured it all in high heels.

"A pretty typical Saturday. There aren't usually events of this magnitude during the week, so that's when I catch up on all the office stuff. Thank God for Shannon to keep me organized. The events themselves are all different—and some of my clients are more challenging than Bex and Eli—but I've gotten to know a lot of the vendors. When you already have a solid working relationship, things tend to go smoothly. This is only the second time I've used that caterer, but the florist and I are in the middle of planning center-pieces for a high tea. And Luther, the DJ, is my go-to guy. I love him."

Daniel felt a sudden irrational surge of dislike for Luther the DJ. "Thinking about your schedule, I'm feeling like a slacker for only teaching three class sections a week. Of course, there's also researching and writing, which can be more grueling than you would think." He carried two glasses of ice water to the living room. "And, recently, a lot of committee work in my attempt to earn tenure."

"Eli mentioned that you should hear in a couple of weeks."

"'Mentioned,' huh? Is that your diplomatic way of saying he was bitching about my preoccupation with it? I'll have you know, during this past week, I haven't obsessed at all." At least, not about his job.

"Why were you so keyed up about it before?" she asked, sipping her water. "From what Eli said, you're a shoo-in."

"He's being loyal. There are several strong candidates for the regents to vote on. It's not just about my being qualified, it's about my beating out someone else's qualifications. As for why I'm so hung up on getting it this year," he said, "it's a little bit about saving face with my family. They're all overachievers who lament my lack of ambition. And the last real time I spent with them was right after Felicity dumped me."

She ducked her gaze, but not before he saw her expression change, pinched and very un-Mia-like. "I didn't realize until today that the two of you were almost engaged."

"I think it only qualifies as 'almost' if she'd actually considered it before turning me down. It was more like she yelled no over her shoulder while sprinting out of my parents' house."

The corner of Mia's mouth lifted in acknowledgment of the visual but her voice was serious when she asked, "Do you miss her?"

The degree to which he did *not* miss Felicity only proved that he'd had no business asking her to marry him in the first place and would make him seem shallow and fickle. "Not exactly," he hedged. Having known her for most of his life, her absence was unfamiliar, but he didn't miss her in the romantic sense. Was there a way to say that without sounding like an ass?

"Forget I asked," Mia said, standing. "It's been a long day and I don't really want to discuss past relationships. I'm exhausted."

He rose, too. "On a scale of one to not-tonight-dear, just how exhausted are we talking?" While waiting for her answer, he unbuttoned her jacket. Whatever happened next, she couldn't very well sleep in a suit. By removing the coat and reaching around her waist to the zipper of her skirt, he was simply helping her conserve energy.

Her impish smile didn't look fatigued. "Probably too exhausted to walk down the hallway." Letting her skirt fall, she pulled her blouse up over her head. "Last night, you said something about carrying me to bed?"

He scooped her up so abruptly she gave a squeak of surprise, then he strode toward his room. After stealing a quick kiss, he set her on the mattress, surprised at how intensely satisfying it was to have her there in his room, in *his* bed, where he could wake up to the sight of her dark hair fanned across the pillow, to her scent on the sheets. He scrambled out of his shirt and slacks, her hungry gaze adding to his hurry. Women had found him attractive before. But Mia made him feel wanted in a way he'd never experienced, her eyes shimmering with such sensual appreciation that he knew he was the luckiest bastard in the world.

Completely naked, he fell across her and they kissed again, a deep, slow tangle of tongues. He reached behind her to unclasp her bra. As stunning as she looked in lingerie, nothing she covered her body with could be as exquisite as Mia herself.

"Gorgeous." He trailed a finger over the swell of her breast, and she moved his hand to cover her nipple. Laughter rumbled through him as he plucked at the tight bud. "Gorgeous and impatient."

She raked her nails up his arms. "Impatient for your mouth on me. After those things you texted last night…" She flushed, obviously aroused by the memory.

That makes two of us. He'd made promises he couldn't wait to fulfill. Plumping her breasts together in his hands, he licked one nipple as his fingers toyed with the other. She was stiff against his tongue, writhing beneath him and making the sexiest noises low in her throat. He turned his head, alternating to the other side, sucking hard. When he tugged gently with his teeth, she responded with a hiss of breath, her back arching off the mattress.

Her hand found his shoulder, and it took him a moment to realize she was trying to push him away.

Confused, he lifted his head. "Don't tell me I have to stop." He punctuated his sentence with another stroke of his tongue against a rigid peak.

"Mmm. No, don't stop. Just roll over." She moved so that she was on her side facing him, giving her better access to slide a hand down between them. Her fingers grazed his abdomen, seeking lower and lower. He forgot to breathe as she circled the head of his erection, thumbing the slit there before clasping him in her fist. She pumped her hand, and his hips rocked of their own accord.

"So hard," she murmured.

"Every damn time I look at you." He lowered his head back to her breast, wanting to make her crazy for him. He was beyond crazy for her. Every stroke of her hand over his shaft was agonizing ecstasy; he wanted her to keep touching him forever.

But if she kept up that rhythm, forever might arrive too soon. So, he tugged her hand away, pulling it to his lips for a quick kiss to her palm. Then he sat up, taking in the sight of her, naked from the waist up, her hair a wild tangle framing that beautiful face. He crooked a finger in the lace band of her panties, tugging them down her supple legs. The silk thigh-highs, he left in place. He traced a path up her thigh until he reached the slippery heat between her legs, finding her wet and ready for him. He groaned, already knowing how good it was going to feel when he drove into that heat.

He reached across her, pausing for a kiss, to get a condom from his nightstand. Once it was in place, he loomed over her, savoring the desire etched in her expression. It was difficult to imagine he could ever get enough of this woman. Gaze holding hers, he pushed slowly forward, and she lifted her hips to meet him, tight and slick around him. Bliss. He withdrew and surged deeper, and it was every bit as good as he'd anticipated, yet he was still greedy for more.

He reached out for one of the smaller pillows at the top of the bed and dragged it beneath her, putting her hips at a more dramatic angle. This time, when he thrust home, she cried out, her inner muscles squeezing in a satiny clench that made his eyes roll back in his head. Her legs wrapped around his waist, anchoring him to her, and she pressed her hands to the headboard behind her, bracing herself as she rocked to meet him over and over.

The bed shook, and he pounded into her, urged on by her breathy cries. His balls tightened, and tension seized his body, the incomparable brutal pleasure of being *right there*, hovering on the precipice of orgasm. Balancing his weight on one arm, he reached his free hand between them, stroking her clit. Her entire body stiffened, then undulated in release. With a growl, he gripped her hips and rode her climax to his own before collapsing atop her, every cell in his being contentedly lethargic.

But he was probably squashing her. He dredged up

enough energy to roll over, keeping her hand tight in his as he lay facedown on the comforter. He turned his head far enough to the side that he could see her, flushed and trying to catch her breath, the portrait of a well-satisfied woman.

She grinned lazily. "I know it's late January. But would you consider turning on your air-conditioning?"

He chuckled. "Give me a minute, I'll get your ice water." He went into the restroom, disposed of the condom and padded naked into the living room. Then he returned with their drinks.

She was stretched out beneath the sheets. "Your bed is very comfortable. Not that I'm complaining about your fetish for sex in public places, but—"

"*My* fetish?" His locked office wasn't public, exactly. And she'd been the one to drag him into that supply room. "I'm too boring to have fetishes."

"For a highly educated man, you're an idiot."

"Ouch." He climbed in next to her. "Remind me to be offended later, when I'm not so mellow from afterglow."

She propped herself up on her elbow, and the sheet fell away from her, dividing his attention between her words and her bare breasts. "I'm a busy woman," she informed him. "I wouldn't waste my time with anyone who bored me. And a boring man would not make me come my brains out in a storage closet."

That startled a laugh out of him even as the memory of going down on her had him semihard again. "Difficult to argue with that logic."

"Don't. You'll save us both a lot of time if you make a habit of accepting that I'm right," she said cheekily.

"Not even the great Mia Hayes can be right all the time. But since it seems rude to argue with a naked woman, I'll give you this one." In a more serious tone, he added, "I'm flattered by your view of me. And grateful." He'd been told to see himself one way for years, had even worked to cultivate that image. Being with Mia was incredibly freeing. He finally felt like his whole self, rather than a carefully edited version that left out some of the most interesting parts.

With a mischievous smile, she set her water aside. "How grateful are you?" she asked, rolling over to straddle his hips. "Because I know an excellent way you could thank me."

He tugged her closer. "By making you come your brains out again?"

"I retract calling you an idiot." She nipped at his lower lip. "You, sir, are a genius."

DANIEL'S EYES OPENED, and the first thing he processed in the dark room was the glowing digital readout of the alarm clock: 4 a.m. *Not again.* But even as the familiar dread began to climb, he hazily registered that something was different. He hadn't been alone when he fell asleep. *Mia.* He turned to the empty side of the bed next to him, then sat bolt upright.

But his confusion was short-lived, dissipating as the bathroom door opened.

She paused a foot from the bed as if trying to make

out his outline. "Daniel?" she whispered. "Sorry if I woke you."

"No problem." At least today, when he couldn't fall back asleep, he'd have the consolation of holding her warm curvy body snug against his.

She slid in next to him, scooting close until she was tucked against his chest. She pressed a soft kiss to his arm and, judging from her breathing, was asleep minutes later. Her lips parted with a dreamy sigh, and a happy lassitude washed through him.

Which was the last thing he remembered until waking up to late morning sunlight and her sleepy smile six hours later.

8

"WELL, *SOMEONE'S* IN a good mood."

Mia turned from the percolating coffeepot in the corner of the reception area to smile at Shannon. "Morning. I didn't hear you come in."

"Probably because you were too busy whistling."

"Was I?" She hadn't realized.

"I've never seen you this cheerful on a Monday." Shannon dropped her stuff off at her desk, then came closer, staring. "I'm not sure I've seen you this cheerful ever."

That couldn't be right. Okay, yes, she'd had a few orgasms over the weekend—a dozen or so toe-curling, bone-melting orgasms—but it wasn't like she'd never had sex before. "Luther was the wedding DJ on Saturday. You know he always plays the best music. Probably just got something stuck in my head."

"Uh-huh." Shannon crossed her arms over her chest, her eyebrows shooting up above her glasses. "And if I pretend to believe that *Luther* is the reason you look like you're about to break into song, do I get some kind of employee bonus?"

"I could take you to lunch."

"Not today, you can't. You're having lunch with Wren and her sister Riley to sign the paperwork for Riley's engagement party, remember?"

"Right!" Mia couldn't wait to see Wren. Not only did she owe her friend exuberant thanks for her part in building Mia's lingerie collection, but Mia wanted to make up for last week's yoga class. At the time, Mia hadn't been in the right frame of mind to join in the other woman's gushing about new romance. Today, she was feeling much more gushable.

She was also in far too good a mood to kick off her day with a sensible protein bar. As many calories as she'd enthusiastically burned over the weekend, why not splurge? "I'm craving pastry."

"Look, boss—" Shannon's tone held a note of warning.

Mia held her hands up in front of her. "I was *not* about to ask you to go get us something in a misguided attempt to throw you in Paige's path. I know you said you'd talk to her when you're ready." But, for Shannon's sake, Mia hoped it was soon. *Why should I be the only one having phenomenal sex?* "I'll run up there. Do you want anything?"

"Anything that's got chocolate works for me."

Mia grabbed some cash and took the elevator up to the café. Paige filled the order with a smile, hesitating for a moment before handing Mia her change, as if she wanted to ask about Shannon but refrained. *Come on, you two*. Mia wondered what it would take to get them in an elevator together and who she'd have to bribe in building maintenance to temporarily cut power. Then she remembered that she was a supportive friend who didn't try to bend others to her will. Dammit.

When she walked back into the office, Shannon was hanging up the phone. "You just missed your father." She said "father" with an unmistakable edge of sympathy, knowing that Mia's relationship with her parents was less than ideal. "I told him you were out but didn't volunteer that you were coming right back."

"Which is one of the many reasons I love you."

Her dad had probably called to lock down details for Valentine's Day. His gift to his wife was bringing Mia's stepmother to the city to see her favorite musical at the Fox Theater. He'd caught Mia off guard by asking her to meet them somewhere for a late dinner, time and place to be determined. She had two events on Valentine's Day, but she'd be finished by eight or so.

And since she hadn't been dating anyone, there'd been no reason to leave the romantic holiday free for her own plans. Could she use Daniel as an excuse to get out of the family dinner? Granted, a torrid weekend in bed wasn't "dating" but she didn't need to give her father specifics.

On some deeply buried level, the part of her that had once been "daddy's girl" balked at the idea of canceling on him. For years, it had just been the two of them, and they'd been close. There were times she truly missed that. The mature thing to do would be to show up at dinner without excuses. *It's one meal before they leave town in the morning. How bad can it be?*

To Shannon, she asked, "I can manage a couple of hours with my parents, right?"

"If I survived breaking the news to my parents that their only daughter was a lesbian, you can sure as hell survive this." It had taken them a few months, but Shannon's parents had eventually become supportive. In their own awkward way.

"Absolutely." Mia squared her shoulders. "I'm going to be a grown-up and go into this with a positive attitude." Still, she found plenty of reasons not to call her father back just yet, staying busy right up until the time when she had to leave the office to meet Wren and Riley.

They'd agreed on a Mexican restaurant close to where Wren worked, so the meeting would easily fit into her lunch break. But even though she was the one with the least distance to travel, she was the last one to show. When Mia arrived, Riley Kendrick was seated at a booth and checking email on her phone. She looked a lot like her younger sister, but her blond hair was shorter, her eyes a clearer blue than Wren's stormy gray.

Mia slid in across from her. "You look great. Being engaged obviously agrees with you."

Riley extended her hand, glancing dreamily at the diamond solitaire engagement ring. "Being engaged is lovely, but being married to Jack will be even better." She said it with such easy confidence, no doubt in her mind that she'd found the perfect man for her.

Mia felt a twinge of something like envy, but brushed it away, impatient with herself. Riley was a wonderful woman who deserved happiness, especially after a rough patch a couple of years ago when she'd been robbed at gunpoint. According to Wren, she'd been agoraphobic for months. "Any idea when your sister will be gracing us with her presence?" Mia asked lightly.

Riley laughed, reaching for the carafe of salsa and filling the empty bowl on the table. "For Wren, anything less than ten minutes late is on time. It always drives our mom crazy, but I think Wren's just trying to cram as much living into her life as she can fit, time constraints be damned."

"That sounds about right."

"I'm here, I'm here, I'm here!" Wren announced her presence from the other side of the partition dividing the dining room before she rushed around the corner. "Sorry." She grabbed a chip as she squeezed in next to her sister. "A friend stopped by the shop to find something sexy for Valentine's Day—she makes wedding cakes, Ry, you should talk to her—and we lost track of time while I was ringing up her purchases."

"Speaking of lingerie purchases," Mia said, "if I don't tell you enough, I really appreciate you including me in your limited number of friends-and-family markdowns. I've, ah, received some compliments lately on my collection."

"From who?" Wren demanded. "You—"

The waitress interrupted to ask if they were ready to order, and they had to admit they hadn't made any decisions. Riley was the only one who'd even opened a menu yet, but she said everything looked so good she couldn't choose.

Wren rolled her eyes. "You know you're getting the burrito ranchero. You always do."

"I was thinking about trying something different this time."

They looked over the selections and were ready when the waitress returned a few moments later. Mia got a fajita salad, Wren asked for the daily special—but made three different substitutions to personalize the dish—and Riley ordered the shrimp tacos. Which she immediately changed to a burrito ranchero.

"Boring," Wren declared.

"I am not," Riley said. "I just know what I like."

"Back me up here, Mia. Tell my sister if she's not careful, she'll end up boring and predictable."

Mia grinned. "You know, sometimes the people you mistakenly think are stuffy or predictable turn out to be…" Seductive. Impulsive. Wickedly talented in bed.

"You have a secret." Wren jabbed a tortilla chip at her in accusation. "Not cool, Hayes. Spill all."

She hesitated, unsure how to sum up Daniel. *I reconnected with a guy who used to bug the hell out of me in college. He's recovering from a very recent breakup by giving me earthshaking orgasms.* "Later," she promised. "Aren't we here on official business? Riley's engagement party first, then my sex life."

Wren's eyes were the size of the decorative sombreros hanging on the wall. "So there *is* actual sex happening? Since when?"

"Since Friday." She sighed at the memory of being in Daniel's office. Someday soon, she was going back so they could take a crack at that desk.

The waitress brought their food out, and Mia was able to steer conversation back to Riley's party. It had been a challenge to find an available date that worked for the people who meant the most to Riley and Jack, but they'd settled on Friday, February 24, at the planetarium. There was a private room for events, and the party would even include a short, customized show.

"I was never a straight-A science student like my sisters," Wren said, "but I did always love the planetarium. Dad used to take me and Riley and Rochelle, then we'd go for ice cream."

"The planetarium's an apt metaphor," Riley said, reminding Mia of Daniel, with his jokes about symbolism and similes in literature. "Before I met Jack, my world had shrunk down to fear and my apartment. In some ways, it's like he gave me back the universe."

"Ugh." Wren mimed banging her head on the table. "I'm deliriously head over heels for Brant, and even *I* find that sickening. Feel free to rave about Jack, but maybe instead of sappy metaphors, you could give us the dirty details of your love life?"

Mia laughed. "What's with all the sudden interest in living vicariously through our sex lives? I thought everything with Brant was smoking hot."

"Best sex I've ever had." But Wren's sigh made the words less than convincing. "We're so attuned. He knows what I like. The only thing is…" She stabbed at her food, frowning. "There's never any sense of surprise, because he does exactly what I would have asked him to. Am I stupid to be disappointed by that? By a guy who gives me what I want? I sound ridiculous."

"Not ridiculous," Mia said. Every time Daniel had taken her by surprise this weekend had been exhilarating. "Familiarity can be comforting, but a touch of the unexpected is…" She stopped, not wanting to make Wren feel worse.

Riley leaned back against the booth. "Jack and I have definitely done things I wouldn't have expected from myself." Judging from her smile, she'd liked those things. A lot.

"Yay!" Wren rubbed her hands together with glee. "Details. Finally."

"There…may be a nude drawing of me somewhere," Riley admitted. "I posed for it on our first date. Then I took him to bed."

Wren gasped. "What the hell did you do for your *second* date? And how do I get a framed copy of that drawing for the engagement party?"

Riley elbowed her in the side.

"Maybe you should try surprising Brant?" Mia suggested. "That could be fun for you and inspire him to reciprocate. You might be astonished what men are capable of with a little encouragement."

Riley nodded. "Rochelle told me when she was trying to get pregnant—"

"Ack, no!" Wren protested. "I've already heard enough about our sister's fertility odyssey to be scarred for life. No one needs to know her brother-in-law's sperm count. Ever. I'm just happy they're finally expecting and look forward to being Cool Aunt Wren."

"Guess that makes me Sensible Aunt Riley, the one who gives our niece or nephew Pepto after hours of junk food in your company."

Wren beamed. "We'll make a hell of a team."

As the waitress cleared their plates away, conversation moved from Rochelle's due date to when Jack and Riley were planning to get married.

"Obviously, we're planning to talk to you about coordinating the wedding," Riley told Mia. "I just figured, one thing at a time."

"The engagement party is a logical audition. If I screw it up," Mia teased, "you have plenty of time to find someone competent before the big day."

"Nothing is getting screwed up," Wren said loyally. "Mia is the best. Except for how she stalled telling me about the new man in her life until my lunch hour was over." She pulled some bills from her gigantic purse. "I have to get back to work. You'd better call me soon."

"I will," Mia promised.

As she was starting her car ten minutes later, her phone rang, and she half expected it was Wren, calling to interrogate. Her friend was not known for patience. But it was Daniel's name on the screen, and her pulse thumped heavy in her chest. She was grinning like an idiot when she activated the Bluetooth. Her affair with Daniel might not be serious, but it certainly made her happy. "Hi."

"Hi." There was an answering smile in his voice. "How's your Monday?"

"Not bad, as Mondays go. But knowing there's no chance of seeing you is putting a damper on my mood." He'd told her he was traveling to a sister campus this evening for meetings all day tomorrow. "I don't know how late it will be when I get back tomorrow night, and I'll probably be brain-dead from trying to care about other people's opinions. But what are the chances I can take you to dinner on Wednesday?"

"Pretty nonexistent. I'm overseeing an anniversary party." A lot of her events were on the weekend, but the couple had been adamant about wanting the celebration on their actual anniversary. "How about Thursday? I'm free after six thirty."

"I'm covering a night class for a fellow professor. Friday?"

"Sorry. I'm booked all weekend." The regret she felt was ironic; after all, a busy schedule meant her business was doing well. "What time exactly is the class Thursday night?"

"Seven thirty to nine."

"How would you feel about a late dinner? I could cook," she offered, surprised by the words. She barely cooked for herself, much less guests—at least, not ones she actually liked.

"Sounds perfect."

Yeah, he said that now. Before he'd tasted anything. Mia frequently got impatient while cooking and rushed through steps or tried to make do with recipe substitutions when she lacked ingredients like crème fraiche or hoisin or jicama. *So keep it simple.* If twelve-year-olds in home ec classes could cook meals, Mia could damn well prepare something. Besides, the devil on her shoulder reminded her, dining privately meant she wasn't limited by conventional wardrobe options. She could swing by Wren's store between now and Thursday and with any luck, Daniel would be too distracted to notice if the pasta was rubbery or the sauce had a slightly burned undertone.

"Then I'll see you Thursday. Thanks for being flexible," she said, grateful for the compromise. "My crazy schedule has been an issue with past boyfriends. Not that you're my... I just mean, I appreciate your understanding."

"Your job's as important to you as mine is to me." His matter-of-fact acceptance was one of the many things she appreciated about him. "I'm not going to get bent out of shape just because I have to wait a few extra days to see you again."

She grinned inwardly, already making plans. "I'll do my best to be worth of the wait."

As Mia opened the door, the words "I brought wine" rose to Daniel's lips but came out an unintelligible splutter as he registered what she was wearing—a deep purple microdress with thin straps, made of stretchy patterned lace that hid very little. A piece of lingerie meant for the bedroom, except that he was fortunate enough to be dating a nonconformist. He got a tantalizing glimpse of full breasts, her nipples barely covered, and swallowed hard.

"Nice to see you, too." She flashed him a mischievous smile, tugging him inside so that she could close the door. When she took the bottle of Cabernet and turned toward the kitchen, he realized that she also wore a matching thong. Even after she disappeared around the corner, the sight lingered like an afterimage of staring at the sun. Only a fool would blink it away.

He followed her, standing in the doorway as she uncorked the Cabernet. The kitchen was small, currently filled with the aroma of pot roast from the slow-cooker on the counter, but he liked the coziness, enjoyed being this close to her and watching the lithe stretch of her body as she reached overhead for wineglasses. Her hair was swept into a casual knot off her neck, which would have guaranteed his being turned on if he weren't already, and her manicure and pedicure were the same deep violet as the lace.

"More lingerie from Wren?" he asked once he'd found his voice.

She turned to face him, nodding.

"I'm going to need her address. To send her flowers."

Mia laughed, parts of her bouncing gently beneath the lace in a way that made his dick swell. "I'm not sure her boyfriend would appreciate that, but I'll introduce you to her sometime soon so you can thank her in person." She held up the bottle she'd opened. "This is pretty swanky. I've never tried it myself, but I've seen it listed on menus."

He shrugged self-consciously. "It's one of the labels I'm familiar with." His parents, who collected for their wine cellar, acted like anything under forty dollars might as well be poured straight out of a box.

She set the bottle on the counter and closed the distance between them with a few short steps, the playful glint in her eyes as alluring as her outfit. "I assume we should let it breathe. I wonder how we could pass the time?" She traced her index finger over the curve of his upper lip and leaned close enough for him to get a hit of her spiced vanilla body lotion. "Oh, I know... You could set the table while I toss the salad."

He groaned out a laugh. "You're a cruel woman."

She fluttered her lashes at him. "Plates are in that cabinet by the fridge."

"Okay. But *I* get to pick the after-dinner activity."

IT HAD TAKEN most of dinner before he'd been able to tear his gaze away from the beautiful, barely dressed woman across from him, but Daniel was finally studying his surroundings. None of the furniture was precisely matched, but it was mostly of decent quality, and she'd decorated with eclectic artwork and bright pops of color.

"I like your place," he told her. "At least, what I've seen of it." He was hoping for the grand tour of the bedroom shortly. Although the leather couch would work just fine, too. Or, for that matter—

"You pretty much have seen it. Only things left are my room and bathroom. It's modest digs."

"Modest, but inviting."

She grinned. "That's the glass of wine and dim lighting talking. You think all these electric candles are for ambience? They cast my housekeeping skills in a flattering light."

He liked that she thought about details like the lighting. This week he'd spent entirely too much time in meetings, and he'd been surrounded by Idea People who'd spoken at length about big new goals for the university. Daniel applauded goals. Yet when challenged on how manpower or resources could be stretched to realistically meet those goals, those same people were at a loss. He'd realized that none of them wanted to bother with details. While party-planning and higher education were very different things, hearing Mia talk about everything from music selection to napkins made him respect her loving attention to what others would consider minutiae. All those little intricacies added up to memorable overall impressions.

"You're very good at your job," he told her suddenly. "I wish more of the people I worked with were like you. Everyone wants credit for big projects, but no one wants to do the grunt work to make them happen." Mia was unafraid of hard work. At Bex and Eli's wedding, she'd been the first one to show up at the solarium and the last one to leave.

She leaned dangerously forward, her cleavage testing the limits of her lacy lingerie, and he thought she was going to say something flirtatious in response. But she stopped herself, her expression turning cautious. "About my job. I'm dying to plan something special for your birthday next week."

His gaze was still on her spectacular breasts. "I'm all yours."

She balled up a napkin and tossed it at him. "Not sex. Well," she added after a brief pause, "not *just* sex.

An actual celebration with actual people before we get to the sex."

"How many people?"

"For the celebration or the sex?" she teased. Then she flashed a reassuring smile. "Don't worry, I'm aware crowds aren't your thing. Do you trust me to plan something you'll enjoy?"

"Yes." He didn't even have to think about it. When had he become so sure of her?

"That's a relief, since I've started tentatively planning it. There's only one small problem. For what I had in mind to work, it would have to be on your actual birthday. You mentioned once that if you didn't spend it with your family, they'd disown you. I assume you were kidding, but…"

"Exaggerating, perhaps, but not wholly kidding. My mother arranges family dinners. My brother Paul managed to miss a few, going to law school out of state and getting the flu one year. Lucky bastard."

"I don't suppose you feel like you might be coming down with something?" she asked with a wink.

He grinned at the idea of telling his family he was too sick to show up. With his luck, his mother would send the housekeeper with homemade soup.

Mia reached for her wine, expression pensive. "I'm not trying to cause trouble. Much. But the way you talk about these people… Do you enjoy spending time with them?"

He took a beat to consider her question rather than blurt out a glib answer. "I love my family. They love me. But their love comes with a lot of expectation."

The pressure to succeed in their household had been oppressive, smothering any sense of fun or silly bonding. "Birthdays with them aren't exactly joyous occasions, they're more like progress reports, where you explain what you've accomplished over the last year of your life."

"Screw that." She looked annoyed on his behalf. "It's *your* birthday. You should have the power to reschedule. Why not have actual fun on your big day and subject yourself to the Keegan Inquisition on another night?"

He chuckled. "If only it were that simple." But as he said the words, a bolt of rebellious zeal shot through him. He was a grown man. Why *couldn't* it be that simple? His mother would be disappointed, and his father would grumble about duty to family. But they were already disappointed that he hadn't managed to hang on to Felicity and that he'd ducked a future in law while they'd been so hyperfocused on grooming his brothers. Next to his disgraced uncle, Daniel was possibly the biggest disappointment of the Keegan family. Instead of trying to fly under the radar or win them over with tenure, why not just embrace it?

Eli and Sean and Mia had all made passing comments about how it might be healthy to lose control every once in a while. Maybe they had it wrong. Maybe what Daniel really needed was to *take* control of his own life and stop letting his family influence so much. It was a heady thought.

Mia stood and picked up her plate. "Give me a few minutes to clean the dishes. Then we'll finish off the wine and discuss your ideas for our 'after-dinner activity.'"

"Want some help?"

"No. Let me do my hostess thing, you just sit and think about what I said." She cupped the side of his face, her expression more tender than he'd ever seen it. Or maybe that was a trick of the candlelight. "I won't pretend to understand your family dynamics, but it's hard not to want more for you. Especially on a day that should be all about you."

All about him? What a euphorically selfish idea. It had been drilled into him that he should care about his family first, about how everything reflected on them, about how mistakes could make his older brothers look bad so Daniel had better not make any. Giddy from Mia's liberating influence, he reached for his cellphone before he changed his mind. His parents wouldn't be asleep; they never missed the late night news.

His father answered on the first ring. "Daniel. Unexpected to hear from you at this hour." His tone was full of rebuke; he didn't even stop to ask why his son was calling.

"Sorry. Had you turned in for the evening?"

"No, no. Your mother and I are just about to watch the news."

"I won't keep you long. I just wanted to let you know I need to reschedule dinner next Thursday."

"Thursday? But that's your birthday."

"Exactly. And I have birthday plans."

"Nonsense." His voice grew muffled as he turned to relate the situation to his wife, who took the phone.

"Daniel?" Sylvia Keegan's voice was perplexed. "I think your father's confused. Why would we cancel your birthday dinner? It's the perfect time for the whole family to strategize—"

"Not cancel, just reschedule." Never mind that some people thought birthdays should be about celebration and cake rather than political strategy.

"But we always get together on your birthday."

"Mom. In thirty-one years of birthdays, did you ever ask me if that's what I wanted?"

"Well, that's gratitude for you! I can't believe that after—"

"We can reschedule it to a night of your convenience, or we can cancel it outright. I love you either way, but I'm following my own plans."

She huffed out a breath, making it clear that Daniel had just annihilated whatever slim chance he'd had of becoming her favorite son. Unless either of his brothers were stupid enough to become embroiled in some kind of sex and drugs scandal. "Wednesday, then." Her icy tone dared him to say that Wednesday was no good for him.

"I'll be there." He grinned at Mia, who was watching with wide eyes from the doorway. "And I'm bringing a date."

9

"You did it." Mia didn't mean to sound so incredulous, but she'd expected him to think over her proposition, not jump on the phone immediately and derail a tradition over three decades old. *Never underestimate the persuasive power of a woman in see-through lace.* "That's terrific. About that part where you said you were bringing a date…" She didn't want to leap to the conclusion that he meant her without getting clarification.

"Ah. Yes, about that." His smile was sheepish. "I was riding the high of speaking my mind. I didn't mean to drag you into meeting my family without asking you first. I don't even know if you're free next Wednesday. Regardless, I can always tell them you had a scheduling conflict and go alone."

As the person who'd urged him to make the call in the first place, she felt like she should help him face the consequences. On the other hand, much as she cared about Daniel, she emphatically did not want to spend the evening with his parents. *Hell, I don't even want to spend an evening with* my *parents.*

The germ of an idea took hold. Her father and step-mother would be here in a couple of weeks. One reason she disliked spending time with them was the suffocating sense that they were ganging up on her, the two of them together finding more fault with her than her father alone ever had. But if she brought a date with her, it would even up the numbers and perhaps put them on good behavior. Surely they'd rein in the usual criticism in front of a stranger.

"My father is bringing my stepmother to town for Valentine's Day. They're taking in a show, and I'm supposed to meet them afterward. How about we trade off moral support? I'll go with you if you go with me."

"Is that your way of asking me to be your Valentine?"

"Or my designated driver." Her lips twisted. "Sometimes I deal with my stepmother better after a few glasses of wine."

"I'm happy to be both. And speaking of wine." He topped off both of their glasses and carried them to the couch, where she joined him. "A toast to you. For giving me the swift kick in the ass I needed."

She laughed. "I keep trying to tell Shannon, swift kicks are one of my specialties."

They clinked their glasses together, and she stretched her legs across his lap as quiet settled over the candlelit room. She'd coordinated several weddings and now found herself wondering about the couples who'd gotten married. Was this how their days ended?

Amiably bitching about jobs and family before lapsing into peaceful physical closeness? For a disconcerting moment, this felt more intimate than when he touched her, than when he was inside her. Uncomfortable, she cast about for something to say just to break the silence, relief bubbling up when Daniel spoke instead.

"So do I get any hints about my birthday?" he asked.

"Nope. It's a surprise." Slowly rotating her ankle so that her foot pressed against him, she gave him a wicked smile. "Although, whether or not the after-party includes birthday spankings is up for discussion."

He blinked, but a split second later, he grinned, matching her tone. "Maybe we should have that discussion this weekend. Via text."

Mercy. The memory of their last texting session left her flushed. "Perv," she said affectionately.

"Says the woman who brought up spanking." He pressed his thumb into the arch of her foot, massaging with such perfect pressure that she moaned, her head falling back against the arm of the sofa. "This is where you were the night we talked on the phone, isn't it? On this couch?" His voice was rougher now, the playfulness gone as his fingers trailed up from her foot to the curve of her calf then across the ultrasensitive skin on the back of her knee.

"Yes." She closed her eyes, remembering—not her own frantic touches there in the living room but his hoarse cry on the other end of the phone. Daniel in the full throes of passion. She shifted her hips, the fabric of her thong growing damp.

He leaned over her, his hand now grazing the tattoo

at the top of her inner thigh. "Would you like to show me to your room, or should I take you right here?"

She trembled with anticipation. If they stayed here, he could be inside her in minutes. But there was lots of space to roll around on her bed and the slatted headboard made for a sturdy anchor.

"I'll take you any way I can get you," he added, "but if you walk down the hallway, I get to watch your ass."

She sat up slowly, his gaze hot on her body. "Follow me, then."

He'd kicked off his shoes earlier. Now, covering the short distance to her bedroom, he shrugged out of his clothes, letting them fall where they may. By the time he pressed her back to the mattress and dotted kisses along her mouth, her neck and the valley of her cleavage, he was gloriously naked.

"Efficient," she said, nipping at his throat. "I like it."

They'd sprawled across the bed with his thigh between her legs, and she ground against him shamelessly while he tugged down the lace neckline hard enough to make her breasts bounce free. He plucked at the straps of the chemise but left them in place.

"I like seeing you framed like this." His eyes were darker than she'd ever seen them, gratifyingly possessive in a way that made her ache. "On display for me."

"I *did* choose this outfit with you in mind."

"Good choice." He rewarded her by lightly rubbing his jaw over one tight nipple, the faint abrasion of his five o'clock shadow making her breath catch. Then he soothed a kiss over her and sucked gently. Too gently, making her yearn for more.

She twined her fingers in his dark hair, trying to arch up against his mouth.

"In a hurry?" he asked with a lazy smile.

"Not at all," she lied. "Go as slow as you like." Holy hell, what was she saying? What if Daniel took her at her word, tormenting her with light caresses and soft kisses? Desire flared higher even as she hoped he didn't. Or maybe she hoped he would. It was all a tangle of need and heat and the throb building inside her that demanded to be eased.

Meeting her eyes, he teased a fingertip over her other nipple. Then twisted, the sudden pressure making her gasp, her toes curling into the comforter as her body bowed upward. His expression was pure sin. "I know how you like surprises."

"You—" Words eluded her, so she squirmed against his thigh again, trying to relieve some of the ache, marveling that in a week's time, she'd tumbled from a bout of extended celibacy to being in the sculpted arms of a criminally seductive lover. She smoothed her hand over his face, sighing. *"You."* It was a rather inane endearment, but he seemed pleased with it, kissing each of her fingertips before scooting lower on the bed to remove the now soaked thong she wore.

"Condoms?" he growled.

"Nightstand." Right next to the clear plastic case holding—

His eyebrows raised as he held up the bullet-shaped vibrator that fit easily in his palm. "Is this what I think it is?" Apparently the heat that bloomed in her face was answer enough. He nodded to himself, studying it. "It's small."

"Gets the job done." There was another, more *traditionally* shaped vibrator farther back in the drawer, but the one in Daniel's hand was meant for clitoral stimulation.

Daniel tossed the condom *and* the vibe onto the bed next to her, then returned to lavishing her breasts with attention. He didn't stop until she was thrashing beneath him, babbling incoherent praise for his mouth, his hands, his cock pressed against her hip in rock-hard promise. Only then did he sheathe himself in the condom.

He reached for the vibrator. "This goes here—" a whimper-inducing brush of his thumb against her swollen clit "—right?"

Unable to find her voice, she nodded.

Pressing his body to hers, he flexed his hips and surged into her in one smooth stroke. His blasphemous curse sounded almost reverent the way he whispered it. She tightened around him, greedy, aroused, but he didn't move. Instead he held her impaled, pinned in place, as he flipped on the little vibe and set it against her, between them. The sensations against her clit, combined with him so deeply inside her, sent her into a frenzy, gyrating and sliding along his length, riding him from below, as her nails scored his skin.

Oh, God. Too much, too much. And, paradoxically, not enough. Not yet. Tension coiled inside her, building, doubling back on itself, approaching a cataclysmic breaking point. Blood swelled to her already engorged nipples, and her hips jerked in a rhythm beyond her control.

"That's it, honey." His tone was stark need. "Come all over me."

She didn't just come. She shattered.

Her guttural cry rang in her ears, and she convulsed around him. When the first tremors shook her, he tossed the vibrator aside and began to piston into her. The world blurred, and she focused on the harsh masculine beauty of his face as his own pleasure climbed and propelled him into shuddering in release.

He fell against the pillows, pitching onto his side to take her with him.

She swallowed back a sudden wave of emotion, startled by the sudden burn in the back of her throat. She should be euphoric, flying. But mixed in with the rapturous satisfaction was also a stab of panic. Every time they had sex, she couldn't imagine it getting any better. It always did.

And it always left her feeling even closer to him than before, inexorably bonded. Whether she wanted to be or not.

MIA STARED THROUGH the windshield, transfixed as Daniel drove onto a curved driveway that was longer than the street she'd lived on as a kid. She wasn't sure precisely where the dividing line fell between *big damn house* and actual *mansion*. But the Keegan family home was, at the very least, mansion-esque. *Mansion lite?* The sweeping front lawn—which included a fountain burbling in the muted glare of twin spotlights—boasted lush grass and full topiaries one didn't normally associate with February. No doubt his parents relied on a team of gardeners. Or ritual sacrifice.

"Do either of your brothers still live at home?" she asked.

"Of course not."

So a house where only two people lived had a three-car garage? At her apartment complex, she didn't even have a dedicated parking spot. The columns in front of the multilevel minimansion made her think of barred windows. She felt trapped and she hadn't even set foot inside. *Maybe it won't be so bad.* Just because her own parents disapproved of her didn't mean his automatically would.

"Paul and Rachel live in Alpharetta with their sons," Daniel was saying. "Paul's a Fulton County superior court judge. Greg's the oldest, the one who hopes to be governor. He and his wife, Ann, have boys, too. Plenty of grandsons to carry on the Keegan family name." He said that part almost grimly. If his proposal to Felicity had gone according to plan, they might have set a wedding date by now. Did it gall him that he was no closer to marriage and a family of his own?

He parked the car. "I owe you for this. But at least you're guaranteed good food. Dinner is always the birthday person's childhood favorite."

"And in your case, that would be…?"

"Seafood risotto."

She stared. Had the Keegans never heard of fried chicken? "You're kidding." She was glad she hadn't realized what kind of meals he was used to when she'd braved cooking for him last week.

"What do you have against seafood risotto?"

"Nothing at all. But I'm a grown woman with a refined palate. *That* was your childhood favorite?"

"It was creamy and comforting."

"So is mac and cheese." She entertained a fantasy of sending his parents a case of it, artificial orange powder and all. *What am I* doing *here?* But she knew the answer to that. Daniel had asked her, so she'd said yes.

Yes was practically her favorite word where he was concerned. She'd certainly shouted it enough Monday night, when he'd come over after work to ostensibly watch a movie. They never made it past the opening credits.

He opened his car door, giving her a reassuring smile. "I forgot to mention, you look beautiful."

She smoothed a hand over the hem of her skirt. Deciding what to wear had been a challenge, but she'd decided it was impossible to go wrong with a classic little black dress. Hers was a vintage organza with lace detailing at the top. Under direct light, the fabric was beginning to show its age, but she filled out the dress nicely and had accessorized with bright, funky jewelry. "Thank you."

Hand in hand, they walked to the front door, which opened while the doorbell was still gonging. A fifty-something woman with a smart haircut and expensive tailored pantsuit smiled up at them. "Daniel!" She leaned close for a fleeting hug. "Happy birthday, my boy." Then she turned to Mia. "And you must be…"

"Mia Hayes. A pleasure to meet you, Mrs. Keegan."

"Oh, dear me, no." An icy voice sounded from the left of the doorway, beyond where Mia could see. But then a woman with alabaster skin preternaturally devoid of wrinkles, white-blond hair and pale gray eyes stepped into view; she looked like frostbite in designer shoes. "That's our housekeeper, Betty. *I'm* Sylvia Keegan."

"I'm sorry," Mia said, her gaze flitting from Betty to Daniel to his mother. She wasn't entirely sure which of the three of them she was apologizing to.

Betty patted her arm with a sympathetic smile. After taking their coats, the housekeeper faded out of the foyer, making herself scarce with such elegance that it was like a magic trick.

"Everyone else is gathered in the dining room already," Mrs. Keegan said, somehow managing to make it sound as if they were tardy. They'd arrived exactly on time.

Mrs. Keegan led them down a tiled hallway. The dining room was dominated by an ornate wooden table big enough to seat fourteen, but only six were there now. Daniel had mentioned earlier that these dinners were adults only. Mia doubted his nephews were disappointed, but what did she know? Maybe they had a yen for seafood risotto.

"Ah, the guest of honor!" a silver-haired man at the head of the table boomed. His face had softened with age, but it was clear all three of his sons had inherited their jaws and cheekbones from him. "And you brought a friend. I can't remember the last time anyone other than family attended one of these dinners."

"Well, except for Felicity," Mrs. Keegan said as she slid into a chair. "But we've always considered her family."

Daniel stilled, a frown on his face, but then smoothed his expression and introduced Mia to Paul and Greg, stern-faced men who would have been quite handsome if they bothered to smile, and their wives, a petite red-head and a petite blonde who looked like they shopped at the same department store.

The redhead, Rachel, was soft-spoken but welcoming. "Lovely to make your acquaintance. And your dress is charming."

"Such a blast from the past," Mrs. Keegan murmured, eyeing the retro dress as if it was something Mia had pulled from a Dumpster. "She looks like an extra from that TV show—the period piece?"

"Downton Abbey?" Mia asked sarcastically.

Mrs. Keegan scowled. "The one with the advertising agency."

"Well, I think she looks beautiful," Daniel said, pulling out a chair for Mia.

She was seated between him and Rachel but directly across the table from Mrs. Keegan. Given the older woman's scrutiny, it was tempting to go see if Betty needed any help in the kitchen.

Almost as if summoned by Mia's thoughts, Betty came into the room with a delicately edged serving platter. "Dinner will be ready shortly," she said. "In the meantime, I hope you'll all enjoy the appetizer—

thin sliced salmon tartare with pureed beets on toasted baguette."

Just like Granny used to make.

In addition to goblets of ice water, all of the place settings included wineglasses; only Daniel's and Mia's were empty. He nodded toward the ice bucket in the middle of the table. "Can I pour you some?"

"It's a well-oaked Chardonnay," Mr. Keegan said proudly, "one of the best vintages in our collection. Unless you're like Rachel?" he added in an aggrieved tone.

Mia turned a quizzical expression to the woman.

"Afraid I only like the dessert wines." She nodded to another ice bucket sitting over on a side table. "You can have a glass of mine, if you enjoy Rieslings."

"I'd love some," Mia said impulsively. Truthfully, sweet wines weren't her favorite, but she disliked the hint of condescension in Mr. Keegan's tone when he'd mentioned his daughter-in-law. God forbid she wasn't sophisticated enough to enjoy wine that tasted like an oak tree. And Rachel had to put up with these people regularly? Mia hoped Daniel's brother was good enough in bed to compensate.

"You know who was very educated about fine wines?" Mrs. Keegan mused as Daniel got up to fill Mia's glass. "Felicity. She—"

"Mother." Greg interrupted her, but his tone was more amused than rebuking. "I think you'll have to accept that she is not currently Daniel's companion of choice."

Currently? A hell of a thing to say in front of Daniel's date. Weren't these people supposed to be painfully polite? So far, she was only finding them painful.

She took the glass of wine Daniel handed her, battling the impulse to chug it. *Pace yourself.* This could be a very long night.

As DANIEL ACCEPTED the silver boat of Betty's homemade salad dressing being passed around the table, Rachel caught his gaze, subtly rolling her eyes at something his mother had just said. Truthfully, Daniel hadn't been listening. He'd been distracted ever since hearing Felicity's name earlier. Until that moment, he hadn't realized that this was the first time he'd ever brought a woman to meet his family. With Felicity, there'd never been a need for introductions, since his family had known hers for years.

During his university years, when he and Felicity had been maintaining a long-distance relationship from separate campuses, they'd agreed it might be good for them to date other people—although they'd found their way back together after graduation, due in part to nudging by their families. Daniel had never brought any of his casual college girlfriends home. Tonight's dinner made Mia special.

She was already special. But he was only just starting to realize how much, and it was jarring. Maybe he shouldn't have brought her here tonight; he could have waited until more time had passed and they had a better defined relationship. He'd told his parents on a whim that he was bringing her without stopping to consider the significance of first impressions.

"So what is it that you do for a living?" Mr. Keegan asked from the end of the table.

"She's a wedding coordinator," Daniel said at the same time Mia answered, "party planner."

"She organized Eli's wedding," he added.

"Oh." Mrs. Keegan smiled. "We sent them a lovely Williams-Sonoma gift set. Are they enjoying their honeymoon?"

Like Eli was calling with daily status reports?

"I also organized Eli's bachelor party," Mia said. For a horrible split second, Daniel was afraid she would tell them about the burlesque show and how she'd been wearing a corset and fishnets when she reentered his life. "I started my business with smaller parties and have been working my way up to big events."

Paul leaned back in his chair. "I never thought of throwing together a party as something that constituted an actual business. Betty's always handled our gatherings, from birthday dinners to holiday galas."

"I guess it's good for my job security that not everyone has a Betty," Mia said.

"Well." Mrs. Keegan gave her son an indulgently chiding glance. "We hardly 'threw together' your wedding to Rachel. It was covered in magazines, for goodness' sake. Speaking of which…" She turned to Greg. "I meant to ask how your interview yesterday went?"

They chatted about his "talking points" and analyzed his main competition in the gubernatorial race. It was a conversation Daniel had heard before and would no doubt sit through again multiple times in the coming months. He didn't realize how far his mind had wandered until his father nudged him with an elbow.

Mr. Keegan repeated his question about whether the tenure position had been awarded yet.

"No, the regents vote in a couple of weeks."

"Well, it doesn't really matter if you get it this time around, does it?" Mr. Keegan asked philosophically. "You'll no doubt be teaching for years to come."

Daniel blinked, telling himself that his father had meant it to be encouraging, a reminder that Daniel still had a long career with plenty of opportunities stretched out ahead of him. Still…he couldn't remember his parents ever telling his older brothers that their achievements didn't matter. Quite the opposite.

Across the table from him, Mrs. Keegan was finishing up some tale about her most recent volunteering efforts. "It's draining, but civic duty is so important, after all. I do hope you take your civic duty seriously," she said to Mia.

"Well, I try not to commit more than one felony a month," Mia said. "I cut myself more slack with misdemeanors."

Daniel sucked in a breath. His parents wouldn't find jokes about criminal activity funny. Before he could say something to dispel the mounting tension, Mr. Keegan injected, "Do you at least vote?"

Mia nodded. "For contestants on singing reality shows *and* dancing ones."

Mrs. Keegan looked appalled, and Daniel dimly remembered that he had once thought it would be entertaining to watch his parents try to cope with Mia's brash personality. *I was wrong.* He'd thought it would be funny because he hadn't realized the stakes would be so high. Caught up in his affair with Mia, reveling in the newness of it and the heat of the moment, he hadn't spared any thought for the future. But it occurred to him now that he wanted Mia and his parents to like each other. Dread tightened in his stomach. *Too late.*

BY THE END of the night, Mia was so eager to leave that she would have willingly sacrificed dessert just to get the hell out of there. Finally, blessedly, it was over and they were taking their jackets from Betty in the foyer. It might be freezing outside, but Mia doubted the most frigid Georgia winter on record could be any colder than Mrs. Keegan's smile as she told Mia goodbye.

God, that was awful. Mia strode down the sidewalk, holding herself back from running to the car. She didn't appreciate the way Daniel's parents talked to him, how they'd treated Rachel, or how they'd rhapsodized over the Virtues of Felicity every three seconds.

Poor Daniel. That was his family's idea of a celebration? Her childhood pets had better birthday parties than that. Literally. She turned to him, about to say she'd had a nice time—as compared to, say, getting a root canal. But she faltered at his shuttered expression and stiff posture. He looked no more prepared to find any humor in tonight than he had in their being busted by Myron like a couple of sophomores.

Okay, silent retreat, it is.

He wordlessly opened her car door. As he got in on his own side of the vehicle, his phone chimed and he removed it from his pocket, scowling at the screen. "My mother," he said flatly.

"Texting to welcome me to the family?"

"Someone who makes cavalier jokes about committing crimes and the importance of voting should not be associated with someone who is running for governor," he read.

She snapped her fingers. "There goes my plan to show up at campaign headquarters and volunteer my services."

"*Mia.*" His voice wasn't loud, but his tone was sharp enough for her to do a double take. "Can you stop?"

She was temporarily stunned speechless, but that wasn't her natural state. By the time they'd rolled through the first traffic light, she'd recovered her words. "I didn't intend for my 'cavalier jokes' to upset you, but joking was my way of surviving that ordeal."

"Maybe it wouldn't have been such an ordeal if you hadn't unleashed all your sarcasm on them."

Déjà vu all over again. She was well acquainted with that judgmental tone of his, and it sent her temper into the red zone. "Are you fucking kidding me? I was *holding back*." She'd thought plenty of things that had gone unsaid. For instance, she'd mildly accepted Mr. Keegan's second offer of Chardonnay instead of retorting that what she really needed was a shot of vodka and the number of a reputable cab company. "I suppose I could have sat there in meek silence and let them treat me like crap, but I didn't want to horn in on *your* strategy." Until the words spilled out of her mouth, she hadn't realized how pissed she was at him.

She'd walked into that room with only one ally, but she'd quickly felt abandoned by him. It seemed like Daniel had checked out of the conversation. "I don't know how Rachel puts up with them." The redhead, who'd muffled laughter at several of Mia's comments, had been the nicest part of the evening.

"Rachel? She's used to my parents. She knows when to take them seriously and when to ignore them."

Was that what he'd expected Mia to do, ignore their derision without standing up for herself? Hell, no. And while she could verbally defend herself, she would have appreciated his support. By his silence, he'd let his family treat her like a subpar placeholder for Felicity or whatever country-club-approved woman he eventually ended up with. "It would have been nice if you'd stuck up for me," she said in a small voice.

He cut his eyes toward her, but she couldn't tell what he was thinking. The man was such an expert at retreating into his shell that he could give lessons to turtles. "I did say I thought you looked beautiful."

Yes. But sticking up for her dress hadn't been quite the same as sticking up for her. Or maybe she just had issues. The betrayal she was feeling now was reminiscent of what she'd experienced when she fully expected her parents' support and they'd responded with roundabout blame instead. Even years later, she felt her parents had been in the wrong. Was Daniel?

She'd known going into dinner that Daniel had his own family issues. She would probably never see those people again, so would it have killed her to bite her tongue for one night? Occasionally, her job as an event planner required her to use tact, whether it came naturally to her or not. Maybe tonight she could have employed a touch more on Daniel's behalf. As an early birthday present.

Yet even as she told herself those things logically, her emotions were a thorny jumble of hurt and anger and self-doubt. When she and Daniel had sex, she felt incredibly connected to him, as if their affair might one day blossom into something more important. But that was the heat of the moment. Tonight he'd been withdrawn to the point of disregard.

What did you expect? She knew this affair was unlikely ever to be more than extremely satisfying casual sex. His being damn good in bed didn't make the two of them any more compatible out of it.

He sighed as they rolled up to her apartment complex. "You probably hate me for taking you there."

"I don't hate you." She almost missed the old college days when she had. What she felt for him now was far more complex. And risky. "In some ways, I might even admire you more. Considering those two glaciers are your parents, it's impressive you turned out half as well as you did."

He gazed out his windshield, not looking at her. "I have my ice cube moments, too."

Yeah. He did. How had she let herself forget that? "And I have my bitchy, abrasive ones."

"You okay?"

"I will be, after a couple of aspirin and a good night's sleep." Alone. There was no need to say the word out loud. At the moment, he seemed to have zero interest in getting any closer to her.

Distance is a good thing, she told herself as she unlocked her apartment door. It would give her desperately needed perspective. And if she couldn't regain it? Then it was time to politely eject Daniel from her life before her feelings became any more complicated.

IT WASN'T UNTIL Mia knocked on the door and her stomach fluttered that she was forced to acknowledge how nervous she was. *Quit overreacting.* Sure, she and Daniel had argued some last night, but they'd shared a couple of friendly texts since then. No hard feelings.

Still, this was his birthday. She wanted it to be perfect for him. If he didn't have fun tonight, then she'd coerced him into rearranging his schedule and antagonizing his parents for no reason other than her own ego. *Be positive.* She'd kept the plans simple and suited to Daniel's tastes. After a few hours out on the town, they'd go back to her place. Where they would enjoy the birthday cake she'd made and hopefully put her mattress's twenty-year warranty to the test.

They hadn't had sex in almost a week. It was ludicrous how much she missed that closeness.

The door swung open, and she barely had a chance to register how good he looked in his blue cable-knit sweater before he'd pulled her to him, his lips slanting over hers. "God, I've missed you," he groaned into her mouth.

Joy lit up inside her. *So maybe not that ludicrous, then.* She kissed him back eagerly, the familiar heat surging, even more potent as desire burned away her earlier nerves. But when his hands dropped to her ass, grinding her against him, she forced herself to disengage.

"Hold that thought, Professor." She truly regretted not scheduling enough time for a quickie in his condo, just to take the edge off. "We have somewhere to be."

He gave her a wolfish smile, bunching up the hem of her skirt, his touch delicate and oh-so-teasing across her sensitive inner thigh. "I know exactly where I want to be."

Yes. Wait, no. Dammit. "Later," she promised breathlessly. She almost kissed him again—just to officially say happy birthday—but was afraid it would leave her brains too scrambled for her to drive.

"Later." He made the word sound deliciously predatory, and she shivered.

By the time they'd reached the parking garage, they'd mostly regained their composure, although the heat in Daniel's gaze as he stole glances at her matched the arousal pulsing through her.

"So you still won't tell me where we're going?" he asked.

"Downtown." She was curious to see if he figured it out as they got closer, unsure if he'd been to their destination before. Eli, who'd returned from his Caribbean honeymoon yesterday morning, had said he couldn't remember Daniel ever mentioning the tavern. Luckily, Eli and Bex hadn't minded Mia intruding on their vacation with a few texts to arrange birthday plans.

By unspoken agreement, Mia and Daniel didn't

discuss Wednesday night or his family. Instead, Daniel amused her with odd tidbits of faculty gossip, and she told him how excited she'd been when Shannon declared a midafternoon break and went upstairs to Paige's café.

"At least she's not avoiding her anymore," Mia said. "I suppose that's a start."

"Be patient. Not everyone is as bold as you are."

"Shannon is the greatest, and I just wish the situation was easier for her."

"Because relationships are typically so easy?" he scoffed. "When was the last time you had one that was simple or effortless?"

The men in her life before Daniel were dim memories at the moment, faded Polaroid snapshots compared to a 3-D movie. "Honestly, it's been so long since I had a relationship, I'm probably not qualified to have an opinion."

"As if you'd let that stop you."

"Definitely not."

They were approaching a hospital parking structure, and when she turned the car, Daniel's eyebrows shot up.

"We're visiting a medical facility for my birthday?"

"No. They allow paid theater parking for across the street." She nodded toward a building with an Elizabethan facade, inspired by the historic Globe Theatre. It stood out enough among the other buildings that she was surprised he hadn't noticed it. Or maybe not so surprised, considering how focused he'd been on her since first kissing her hello. "What kind of self-respecting literature professor has never been to the Shakespeare Tavern? Way better Atlanta landmark than the Hash Brown Hut, I promise."

He laughed. "Not exactly high praise, given your opinion of the Hut, but I do like Shakespeare."

"I know. Which is why I got us tickets to tonight's dinner theater comedy."

Once they'd crossed the street and were shown into the dining room, the second half of his surprise was revealed—the guests. His friend Sean hadn't been able to make it, but Eli and Bex were there. Eli had also helped her track down one of Daniel's college buddies; the guy lived in North Carolina now and had been willing to visit for this and to see his family while he was in town. Daniel looked legitimately shocked and thrilled to see him and his wife.

Originally, Mia had tried to purchase tickets for nights other than Daniel's actual birthday, but the performances had all been sold out. So when she'd stumbled across the opportunity for two four-person tables, she'd snapped up the tickets before she'd even heard back from potential guests. In place of Sean and his date, Mia had invited Wren and Brant; she hoped Daniel wouldn't mind that she'd rounded out the group with her own friend. It made dinner feel more like a party she was attending and less like all the ones she worked, as an outsider rather than a participant.

"Daniel, this is one of my best friends, Wren Kendrick, and her boyfriend, Brant Vaughn."

The two men shook hands, and then Daniel turned to Wren with a twinkle in his eye, squeezing her shoulder in an almost hug. "The famous Wren! I insist you let me buy you a drink. You're one of my favorite people."

Wren giggled. "I understand you're a fan of my taste in store inventory."

Tonight, Daniel seemed to be a fan of just about everything. He was relaxed and prone to laughter, proclaiming the traditional pub food fantastic and calling Mia a genius. Dinner was scheduled so that there was just enough time for all of them to chat and unwind without any worry about running out of conversation before the show started. Eli and Bex showed a few pictures from their honeymoon, and Wren passed out special VIP coupons for discounts at the lingerie store. When the lights dimmed and the director took the stage to welcome everyone, Daniel leaned close to kiss Mia just below her ear.

"Thank you for this," he said. "I can't remember the last time I enjoyed a birthday this much."

Based on what she'd seen last night, the Keegans hadn't offered any real competition. But she refrained from ruining the moment with sarcastic commentary on his family. Instead, she just grinned. "Wait until I take you back to my place." She was working all weekend, so she planned to make the most out of every moment together tonight. "I made you a cake. I've never done that for anyone before."

"You baked?" he whispered skeptically.

"Don't worry, Shannon supervised."

Later, after they'd laughed themselves silly over the play and hugged their friends goodbye, she drove him to her apartment. "There wasn't enough time for the cake to cool completely before I left," she said as she unlocked her front door, "so I didn't have the chance to frost it." She flashed him a meaningful grin. "Want to help me with the frosting, birthday boy?"

"Just so happens, I have a major sweet tooth."

He took her hand and tugged her toward the kitchen, where he lifted her up onto the counter and kissed her with all the craving he'd had to repress for the last four hours. When Mia trembled with the force of her own need, he reached for the plastic tub of frosting.

But, in the end, not much of it wound up on the cake.

10

MIA WOKE IN stages on Sunday morning, emerging from sweet dreams to the even sweeter reality of Daniel nuzzling her neck, his morning scruff a teasing friction against her skin.

Without yet opening her eyes, she laced her fingers through his. "You're actually here. I thought maybe I'd dreamed it." She'd worked last night, but he'd asked her to text him and let him know when she got home safely. After their texts turned heated, he'd crossed town at one in the morning to be with her. They'd made love quickly, not getting any farther than her couch before he was thrusting into her and making her mindless; once they'd hit the bed, she'd been asleep in minutes. Now, she felt well rested, but she was starving.

"You know what would be fantastic right now?" she asked.

His fingers drew invisible loops down her spine. "I have some ideas. What was yours?"

"Breakfast in bed. I'm famished."

"If I make you breakfast, do I get to pick the after-breakfast activity?"

She grinned, recalling his request to pick their after-dinner activity when she'd cooked for him and how that night had turned out. "Enticing. Unfortunately, making me breakfast in this apartment would require that there be actual food in this apartment. This week was crazy-busy, and aside from a few cake supplies, I never got around to any real grocery shopping." Today would be busy, too. She had two client meetings this afternoon and a customized murder mystery party this evening. But she needed to fuel up before she could face any of that. *Food!* And much coffee.

"There's a place not far from here that makes a killer Sunday brunch," Daniel told her.

"I'm not sure I trust your taste," she said suspiciously. "After all, you voluntarily eat at the Hash Brown Hut."

"Oh, no, this place is worlds above the Hut. Galaxies, even. Omelets with just about any produce you can think of, fluffy Belgian waffles, mimosas, a variety of quiche—"

Her stomach gurgled. "What are we waiting for?"

They showered together, stealing kisses beneath the steamy spray, and she slicked her still-damp hair into a casual bun that went well with black jeans and a baggy sweater that was the most comfortable piece of clothing she owned.

Since Daniel was the one who knew where the restaurant was, he drove, seeming almost as eager to dive into brunch as she was. "This is one of my favorites places," he said, pulling into a parking garage. "But I haven't been in forever. Their bacon pancakes are life altering."

"What if they're not on the menu anymore?" she teased.

He slanted her a wounded glance. "Why would you even joke about that?"

"Sorry. Hunger makes me cruel."

Hand in hand, they crossed the street to an upscale café. Obviously, the Sunday brunch was popular. The benches surrounding the hostess stand were packed. Still, the willowy woman with the shaved head assured them the crowd wasn't as bad as it looked and that they should be seated in about ten minutes.

Happily, that proved true. A waiter led them to the table, through a dining room that smelled so delicious Mia's mouth actually watered. Daniel talked her into a decadent combo platter so that she could try a variety of menu items and ordered them a round of Bloody Marys. Her first bite of biscuits and gravy made her eyes roll back in her head.

He grinned from across the table, looking as smug as if he himself had made the food from scratch. "Do I know how to pick a place or what?"

"Yes, you're a genius. Now, be quiet a minute. I'm having a religious experience over here."

Chuckling, he dug into his own sizable breakfast. It was long, contented moments later before he spoke again. "Any chance you've eaten enough that you're feeling mellow and generous?"

Generous? Uh-oh. "I see how it is. Ply a girl with

bacon pancakes, then ask for a favor. Diabolical, Professor."

He winked at her. "I prefer *strategic*."

"For this food, I will grant you just about anything. As long as it doesn't involve dinner with your parents." *Never again.*

"This won't be hostile, just boring as hell."

"You missed your calling as a salesman."

His expression shifted, and vulnerability shone in his gaze. "The college administration is hosting a reception Friday night at the president's house to welcome a new dean. Several of the regents will be there, and it's a chance to see them—my last chance to make a good impression—before they vote on the tenure candidates."

She bit the inside of her lip. Friday? She was scheduled to be on-site at an event, but it wasn't anything too complicated. There was a possibility she could delegate the job to Shannon. She knew how important that board of regents vote was to him, and she'd witnessed firsthand how important networking at social events could be.

He correctly interpreted her hesitation. "You have to work that night, don't you?"

"Maybe. I might be able to rearrange some things," she conceded.

"I'd love to have you with me." He reached for her hand, brushing his thumb across her knuckles. "The moral support would mean a lot. Plus, needless to say, having a woman like you with me would make me look damn good."

She laughed. "I don't think I've—"

"Daniel?" A soft Southern voice came from just behind them. They both looked up to find a trio of blonde women who had to be sisters. The one in the middle, the youngest, was the one who'd spoken.

She was beautiful in an almost surreal way, with wide blue eyes and flawless features. She looked like one of the exquisite antique dolls Mia's stepsister collected.

"Felicity." Daniel's smile was a little awkward, but still genuine.

He rose from his chair and gave her a quick hug while she kissed his cheek. They were a ridiculously attractive couple, the contrasts in their height and coloring striking. Behind Felicity, her sisters exchanged meaningful glances with each other.

One of them suggested, "You and Daniel catch up, we'll meet you at the table." Then they strode away, both texting furiously. The Keegans weren't the only ones who wanted to see Daniel back together with his ex.

"Mia, this is Felicity Green, longtime neighbor and friend of the family. Felicity, this is Mia Hayes, my... friend."

That stung more than it should have, but what else could he have said?

Felicity gave her a sweet smile that was almost shy. "I apologize for the interruption, but I haven't seen Danny in weeks." She turned her gaze back to him, humor lighting those impossibly sapphire eyes.

"I guess we both had the same craving for Sunday brunch."

This was clearly a place they'd frequented when they were together. Understandably. The food was scrumptious. Mia did *not* feel irrationally slighted that he'd taken her somewhere he'd shared with a past lover. This was a public place open to everyone, not a recycled engagement ring. There was nothing to stop her from coming back even after this affair with Daniel had ended.

The brunch that had seemed like heaven five minutes ago now roiled in her stomach. Would it be Mia six months from now, calling hello to Daniel while he dined with a new lover?

She listened with half an ear as Daniel asked Felicity about her job as a CPA, and Felicity laughed that she was fighting the usual struggle of trying to make her clients send her tax information in a timely manner and embrace more organized methods than throwing all their receipts in a shoe box. Then she cast Mia a sympathetic glance. "I'm probably putting you to sleep, aren't I? Nothing makes for more exciting conversation than number crunching," she said with gentle self-deprecation.

"Actually, I realized a couple of years ago that hiring the right accountant made a ton of difference to my company. I have a lot of respect for what you do," Mia said truthfully. "If I had to wade through all of that incomprehensible tax code, my eyeballs would bleed."

"There are days it feels like that." She reached into a designer handbag that probably cost as much as one of Mia's car payments and pulled out a business card. "In case you ever find yourself shopping for a new accountant. Or want to hear any embarrassing middle school stories about Danny."

Mia took the card with a grin.

"I'll bet your job is far more exciting than mine," Felicity said. "I went shopping with Rachel Keegan and she told me all about it."

Mia's smile tightened on her face. She'd really liked Rachel, but Felicity's casual comment reminded her that Daniel's ex fit seamlessly into his family in a way Mia never would. The only reason Felicity wasn't *officially* joining his family was because she'd said no.

Did she regret letting Daniel go? Mia searched the woman's face as she told him goodbye, watching for signs of regret or possessiveness. But Felicity's smile was open and seemed utterly without agenda as she waved to both of them and left to rejoin her sisters.

Daniel's gaze stayed firmly on his plate as he said, unnecessarily, "So, that was Felicity." Was he not meeting her eyes because *he* had emotions he was trying to hide? Or was he trying to scrutinize Mia's reaction without being obvious about it?

"Yeah. I got that." The other woman was a living, breathing reminder that just last month, Daniel had wanted to spend the rest of his life with her. It took time to move on from feelings that strong. "I also get why your family adores her." A sweet-natured woman with sharp intellect and a sense of humor, who'd give them gorgeous grandbabies? "She's damn near perfect."

Daniel glanced over his shoulder in the direction Felicity had gone. "Yeah." He smiled back at Mia. "But imperfect can be a lot of fun."

Right. Fun. She swallowed hard. "Do you miss her?"

He frowned as if confused by the question. "Not really. There's no reason to—Felicity will always be part of my life."

It wasn't quite the answer she'd selfishly hoped for.

"It was awkward," Sean said as he passed the basketball to Eli. Sean's teammate wasn't there yet, and the three of them were warming up.

Daniel raised an eyebrow at his friend's assertion. "*I'm* the one who was there, and I'm telling you, it wasn't awkward at all."

"To run into your ex-girlfriend with your new lover?" Eli asked skeptically. "Sorry, I'm with Sean on this one."

"The three of us had a nice chat. Felicity even gave Mia her card in case she wanted to get in touch sometime."

The ball got away from Sean as he stared. "That's not natural."

"Sure it is. We're all civilized adults. And you know how kindhearted Felicity is," Daniel reminded him. "She may not have wanted to marry me, but she still wants me to be happy."

"So you're okay with her shooting down your proposal?" Eli said. "No…lingering feelings?"

"Not bad ones." The more time that passed, the clearer Daniel could see that his love for Felicity hadn't been based on passion. They'd been…sensible.

On paper, they were the perfect couple. Unlike his relationship with Mia, who approached situations very differently than he did. Still, it was Mia who filled his thoughts and rocked his world. "I invited Mia to the faculty reception," he said.

Sean made a face. "I thought you liked this woman. These receptions are full of boring people."

"Hey." Eli shoved the other man lightly. "I'll be there."

"I didn't mean *you* were boring," Sean said. "I was talking about Daniel."

Daniel ignored the jibe. Mia didn't think he was boring, and that was good enough for him. Under her influence, he was learning to be more spontaneous, to have fun. *And if I want this to be more than casual, naked fun?*

It had only been a few weeks, too soon for anything serious. He didn't want to ruin a good thing—or scare her off—by getting uptight about their relationship. Small steps, he cautioned himself. Never mind that they were about to spend Valentine's Day with her parents or that Daniel had invited her to meet his boss.

MIA DIDN'T ATTEND every event she arranged; sometimes, it was simply a matter of making the necessary reservations for her clients and following up with them later to make sure everything had been to their satisfaction. But the woman who'd called her about putting together a charity event for Valentine's Day was close friends with Penelope Wainwright—Mia's most influential client—and Mia went the extra mile to make sure that everything was perfect for the ball. It was a formal father-daughter dance with pricey tickets that benefited a pediatric cancer center.

The silver lining was, since half the guests were under twelve, the event didn't run very late. On the other hand, by the time she left to pick up Daniel, she was already emotionally raw from watching doting fathers with their adorable little girls. The hurt teen-ager who still lurked deep inside of her wished she was wearing better armor—preferably a leather skirt and a middle finger emoji T-shirt. But she was a mature adult now. Besides, she didn't have time to change, so she'd be arriving in the same emerald green cashmere dress and French braid she'd chosen to look profes-sional at the charity ball.

Probably for the best. They were having dinner at her parents' hotel, which she'd heard had a fabulous ballroom space. Mia planned to introduce herself to the manager on duty, who might be less inclined to work with her if she was sartorially flipping the bird.

As she took the elevator up to Daniel's place, a wave of affection swamped her. Things between them lately had felt very two-steps-forward, one-step-back. She vacillated between believing the tension heralded the inevitable end of their affair and wondering optimis-tically if the strained moments were growing pains leading to a richer relationship. But tonight she was just damn glad he was coming with her.

She appreciated the moral support more than he would ever know. Which was why she'd asked Shan-non to take point on their event Friday night so that Mia was free to attend his university reception. She'd texted him yesterday, and he'd been thrilled. He'd promised that however stuffy it was, he'd make sure their "after-reception activity" was unforgettable.

He answered while she was still knocking, as if he'd been impatient to see her, which made her smile in spite of her trepidation over dinner with her folks.

The sensible pumps she'd worn to work the charity ball didn't have much of a heel, so she raised up on tiptoe to kiss him. "Happy Valentine's Day." She handed him a gift bag. It was a relatively silly token of her regard, but Daniel could use some silly in his life.

He ushered her inside, and she gratefully accepted the stay of execution. "Wait right here," he told her, disappearing around the corner and returning with a bag of his own.

She accepted it with a smile, opening hers first at his urging. Inside was an adorable teddy bear with red horns, a pitchfork and a red cape. Daniel had attached a handwritten note that said, "To My Valentine, who's hot as hell."

She laughed. "Cutest devil I've ever seen. Thank you."

He seemed amused by his gift, too, a book cataloguing Shakespeare's best dirty jokes. "If I used this in class to liven up the material, my students would love me."

Love. Her smile faltered at the word. It would be so unwise to let herself fall that completely for him, but in her honest moments, she wondered if she hadn't already started the plummet. It wasn't as if a person

could just stop midair. *So, now what?* Keep scream-
ing and wait to see if she landed safely in his arms or
in a jagged heap of emotional carnage?

She swallowed. "Ready to go?" *Might as well get
this over with.*

He nodded, but instead of reaching for the keys
that hung on a wall hook a few feet away, he reached
for her. He didn't kiss her, just tucked her against his
broad chest and rested his head atop hers in a moment
of wordless comfort as he reminded her he was there
for her. She squeezed her eyes shut against the sudden
burn of tears. The teddy bear had been a playful expression of an inside joke, but this hug? Best Valentine's Day gift ever.

MIA TURNED DOWN her car radio. "I want to tell you
something." Well, *want* was too strong a word. But it
was as though Daniel's hug had knocked something
loose inside her. She felt compelled to share parts of
herself that she normally kept closely guarded. At any
rate, it seemed only fair that she tell him more about
her history with her dad and stepmother so that he had
a frame of reference for what he was walking into.

"Fire away," he encouraged.

She took a deep breath. "I told you my dad and I had
a falling out. It was because of a single father I used to
babysit for when I was a teenager. The man had been
out later than expected one summer night, and when
his friend dropped him off, he was drunk. Drunker
than I'd ever seen an adult before. I was antsy to drive
home, but his six-year-old had been having nightmares

since the divorce, and I worried his father might not be there for him if he was passed out. The way *my* father was always there for me after my mom died." At one time in her life, she'd idolized her dad. That's what had always hurt the most, not that they hadn't shared a close relationship but that the person closest to her had failed her.

"Anyway, I stuck around to try to get some coffee into the guy and make sure he didn't break his neck trying to go up the stairs to bed. At first, he thanked me, told me how sweet I was, how I would make a much better wife someday than his unfeeling bitch of an ex. Then his comments got more... He cornered me in the kitchen and kissed me." *Kiss* was too pretty a word for the way he'd plunged his tongue in her mouth, tasting like acrid liquor and cigarettes. She'd been too shocked to move at first, although she'd hissed and clawed like a wet cat once he shoved his hand inside her tank top.

"Mia." Daniel's voice shook with rage. "Did he—"

"He was inebriated enough for me to fight him off, especially with the aid of hot coffee." He hadn't thought she was so sweet when she'd scalded him with it; he'd yelled obscenities as she sprinted out of the house and to her stepmother's borrowed car. Afterward, she'd felt guilty for leaving the little boy in the house with an outraged drunk. She'd sent up prayers of gratitude when the boy's mom won full custody a month later. "I was a mess when I got home. In hindsight, I was really too upset to be driving safely. I went straight to my dad and stepmom. They'd already gone to bed for the night. At first, I think they couldn't quite process what I was telling them. But then it was like, they didn't *want* to process it."

"They accused you of lying?"

"Not in so many words. But they questioned whether it was really as awful as I described it or if I'd blown the incident out of proportion in melodramatic teenage hysteria. The guy hadn't been handling his divorce well, but he'd been a member of the community for years. He'd attended barbecues at our house. I think denial was easier for them than accepting that they'd had their daughter's would-be rapist over to play cards. And they kept asking whether I'd said or done anything to encourage him, if I'd flirted or practiced any newfound womanly wiles on him." Insult to injury, in a way that left her second-guessing her own rights and innocent actions.

When she realized how tightly she was gripping the wheel, she tried to do some yoga breathing to lower her blood pressure. "My dad was already nervous about my leaving for college the following summer, and this put him into hyperdrive, lecturing me on all the things I should avoid so I didn't give boys the Wrong Idea, on how I should protect my virtue so I didn't end up with the reputation of campus slut. That wasn't his exact wording." But close enough.

"Hence the chip on your shoulder?" Daniel asked.

"I was furious." And, on some level, she still was.

It was no longer about the horrible babysitting incident. It was about the year of being told she should be more like Patience, who never drew untoward attention. It was about the disappointed sigh of "oh, Mia" when she pulled out a bikini during her first—and last—spring break home from college. It was about the unsolicited advice that parties were not a reputable workplace for a single young woman with an MBA, never mind that she was now in the contact list of one of Atlanta's most respected socialites or that the ball she'd arranged this evening had earned thousands of dollars to help kids with cancer.

"After my mom died, Dad was my world," she said raggedly. "I spent my childhood secure in the knowledge that he was proud of me, my biggest supporter. For him to be ashamed of who I am, to try to change me..." She expelled a gust of air.

"I'm humbled you opened up to me like this," Daniel said carefully. "But I have to admit, hearing all of this right before I'm about to meet the guy may color my opinion of him."

Was that why she'd told him? Were her motivations petty? Did she *want* Daniel to dislike her father on her behalf? Not consciously. "In his limited defense, after he ticked me off, I acted out some. You've met me. I'm sure you can imagine." She'd been trying to prove a point. Or maybe she'd just been trying to see if her father could still love her in spite of her rather dramatic flaws.

"So." Daniel met her eyes fleetingly before she turned her gaze back to the road. "Your family reunions are about as much fun as mine, is what you're saying?"

His wry tone helped soothe her, and she flashed him a grateful smile. "Something like that. I thought you deserved a heads-up in case I get a little…cranky. Tonight might not be a typical Valentine's Day date."

"If I wanted typical, honey, I wouldn't be with you."

They'd arrived at the swanky hotel, a romantic splurge for her parents, and she let the valet take the keys to her car. She was starting to feel jittery. The last thing she wanted to do was accidentally sideswipe someone's Lexus in the parking lot.

Daniel took her hand as they entered the hotel and asked an employee to point them toward the restaurant. Mia tried to remember the last time she'd seen her parents. Most families made a point of visiting around holidays and long weekends, but since those were some of her busiest event-filled times, she had a ready-made excuse not to go home. It had been at least a couple of years since she'd seen her estranged family.

And those years showed in the abundant silver threaded through her dad's dark hair and the new lines around her stepmother's doe-brown eyes as they rose from the table to greet Mia and Daniel.

"Dad, April, this is Daniel Keegan. Daniel, Joseph and April Hayes."

Joseph regarded Daniel with suspicion, which had been how he looked at all of Mia's dates since she'd held hands with a boy on a fourth-grade field trip. But April looked flat-out *delighted* to see him. She actually hugged him instead of shaking his hand.

"So, so nice to meet you," she gushed. "Since Mia rarely visits, we never get to meet any of her…friends from the city."

Mia squirmed at the reminder that she hadn't been

home in years. *Maybe if being there didn't make me feel uncomfortable and judged, you'd see more of me,* she silently told her stepmother.

They all sat, Mia and Daniel on one side, her parents on the other, and her throat closed with all the things she'd wanted to say to them since moving out, both angry and conciliatory. There was just too much of it, and she wouldn't know where to start.

Daniel gamely threw himself into the awkward silence. "How was the musical? I've never seen it, but the Fox always has wonderful performances."

They chatted about the play for a few minutes, and by the time the waitress took their orders, Mia was feeling much calmer. She told them about how she'd planned the wedding that Daniel was best man in, which rekindled their "college friendship." It was a simpler explanation than explaining they'd been college rivals who'd secretly wanted to sleep with each other.

"So your business is doing well?" Joseph asked.

She wished he didn't sound so surprised. "Very. I'm really increasing my client base. I do personal parties like *quinceañeras* and baby showers, but I handle events for organizations, too, like the charity ball earlier tonight."

"I'm so happy for you," April said. "And you've never looked better." She nodded approvingly at Mia's braided hair and cashmere dress before beaming at Daniel. "It's easy to see you've been a good influence on our daughter."

Mia's spine tensed.

Beneath the table, Daniel placed his hand on her

thigh, high enough that, under different circumstances, heat would already be twisting through her. "She was smart, beautiful and successful long before I went out with her. If anything, *she's* influenced *me* to be a better version of myself."

Mia shot him a grateful smile. *You are getting so lucky tonight.*

April cleared her throat. "Maybe, if you had a few days in your schedule to come home, *we* could hire you to do an event, Mia?"

A birthday? Or maybe a milestone anniversary, she thought, trying to do math in her head. "What event is that?"

"Your sister's wedding."

Mia gaped. "Patience is getting married?" She hadn't even known her stepsister was seeing anyone. Granted, she didn't go out of her way to call or email Patience, but communication was a two-way street. *Or in our case, a no-way street.*

"Her engagement is very recent," Joseph said gruffly. "Since we already knew we were coming to Atlanta, she didn't call you. We thought our telling you in person was the next best thing to her telling you face-to-face."

April frowned, toying with the straw in her drink. "I know the two of you were never as close as Joe and I hoped...but maybe that can change now that you both have so much going for you. Her, engaged. You, running your company and dating this handsome fellow."

Daniel smiled at her, but Mia could feel him studying her, trying to process how upset she was. Truthfully, Mia didn't know. Sometimes she felt like an outsider in her own family, but asking her to coordinate Patience's wedding seemed like an olive branch. When dinner was over, she told her parents she'd think over the request and would talk to her stepsister about it.

She was in a strangely vulnerable mood as she and Daniel climbed into her car. "Come home with me?" she asked. She wanted to be in her own environment, but she didn't want to be alone.

"I'd be happy to," he said softly. He also seemed happy to give her some space to sort out her thoughts, not saying much about dinner during their drive. It wasn't until they were turning into her apartment complex that he ventured, "They seem nice. Flawed, maybe, but decent. And for what it's worth, they love you."

"I know." They'd even seemed proud of her, although April, in particular, had seemed more admiring that Mia was with a fine upstanding man than of Mia's individual accomplishments.

"Think you'll do the wedding?" he asked.

"Not without some lengthy discussion with Patience. She's the bride, it should be her decision, not something our parents cooked up to try to bring us closer. Even then…" Trying to pull something together where she didn't know any of the vendors or venues would be different from working here. Not to mention, she'd have to take significant time away from the office.

"You told me before that you regretted going off to college with a chip on your shoulder. There's something to be said for second chances." He gave her an endearingly crooked grin before climbing out of the car. "I'll be eternally grateful that you gave *me* a second chance after I botched our first date."

He wasn't the only one feeling grateful. "You made tonight so much better than it could have been." He'd listened and supported, he'd praised her talents, he'd offered advice that was insightful but not pushy.

"Don't mention it. Just doing my job as your Valentine."

"I know this hasn't been the most romantic Valentine's Day, but I think there's still time to salvage it," she said as she unlocked her front door. "How would you feel about a bubble bath for two?"

"Soapy, naked fun?" He tugged gently on her braid. "Count me in."

She scooped up an armful of electric candles as she passed through the living room. While Daniel went to get towels from the closet, she started the water, pouring in a generous capful of vanilla bubble bath. She'd just pulled off her dress and was reaching behind her to unfasten her bra when his shadow fell across the doorway.

He watched with avid eyes, his voice a low rasp, "Don't stop on my account."

Holding his gaze, she slid the straps of her bra slowly down her arms. Then she turned around to give him a better look as she removed her bikini briefs, bending all the way over to tug them free of her ankles.

Daniel was there in an instant, pressed against her, his hands cupping her breasts as she straightened. He licked the shell of her ear. "The sight of you bent over like that is going to be seared onto my mind for decades to come."

She grinned inwardly at the admiration in his voice. He did know how to make a woman feel sexy. She spun around in the confines of his embrace. "Now we just have to get *you* undressed." She reached for the top button of his black shirt. When she'd popped the first two open, she leaned in to kiss the strong column of his throat. As she bared his chest, she scraped her teeth across a flat nipple, and his hands tightened on her ass.

"More," he breathed.

She did the same to the other side, then dotted kisses toward his navel as his shirt hit the floor behind him. His belt took her a couple of tries, the front of his pants distended by the heavy erection beneath. But finally, she had him unbuckled and unzipped. As she pulled the boxer briefs down, she sank along with them, going to her knees on the cushiony bath mat, running her fingers over his strong thighs and calves, enjoying the slight friction of the coarse hair that dusted his skin.

A glance over her shoulder showed that the bubbles in the tub were more than halfway to the top; any higher, and water would slosh everywhere when they got in. She arched back on her heels, practically a yoga pose, to reach the faucet behind her. Steam rising from the tub curled over her skin.

"We should let it cool," she said, meeting his eyes. "The water's super hot."

"Not as hot as the sight of you kneeling in front of me."

Smiling, she wrapped her hand around the base of

his swollen cock, leaning forward to lick the crown, swirling her tongue and making him hiss out a breath. Lowering her head, she took him as far as she could before her mouth met her hand. She didn't suck him yet, just moved up and down until he was wet and slick. When he subtly bucked his hips, she increased her suction, hollowing her cheeks as she stole a glance up at him. His eyes were closed, his face was rigid, jaw clenched, cheekbones in stark relief. Seeing him that turned on made her feel needy, too. She moaned around him, and he suddenly opened his eyes.

"I have to be inside you." He helped her to her feet.

She grabbed a condom from the medicine cabinet behind him, her heart racing at his expression. How could anyone look so primal and tender at the same time?

There was nothing tender about his kiss as his mouth slanted hungrily against hers. He backed her into the wall, lifting her so that she could wrap her legs around him, settling her entrance over him. "I have the world's sexiest Valentine," he said, flexing his hips and driving up into her.

She couldn't move much, pinned between him and the wall, but oh, holy hell, could she *feel*. Hands on her hips, Daniel worked her ruthlessly up and down his shaft, giving her more pleasure than she could process. When she glanced to the side and caught sight of them reflected in the mirror—his muscles straining, her ankles locked just above his chiseled ass, a sheen of sweat covering them both—the tremors started, small convulsions as she contracted around him, drawing him tighter into her, and then it was a clenching deep in her core as she shook and clung to him for dear life. He had her. Of course, he had her. He'd been proving it all night, with his reassuring touches and words of praise.

I love you. She bit down on her lip until she tasted the faint metallic tang of blood. There'd be no taking those words back, no sense in putting them out there. This was a rebound affair, she told herself as he shuddered to completion in her arms. An intense, currently sticky affair, but not a future that made sense.

He pulled back with a smile of immense satisfaction. "Do we get to relax in the tub now? I'd say we earned it with all that exertion."

She nodded, but even as she returned his smile, she was silently lecturing herself. She advised many a client to be realistic about their budgets for big events. "I will give you the event of your dreams," she'd once promised a woman, "but you need to shape those dreams intelligently." And so did Mia, if she didn't want to get her heart broken.

11

THE PRESIDENT OF the university lived in a two-story house on the south side of campus with a front porch swing, high-ceilinged spacious rooms perfect for job-related entertaining and a balcony overlooking a charming courtyard. Currently, Mia was considering throwing herself off the balcony.

If I land in the koi pond, I might be able to walk away unscathed. It seemed preferable to another five minutes of this party where everyone was intent on sucking up to the three regents in attendance. Daniel's brand of sucking up wasn't quite as cringe worthy as some of his colleagues', but she still wanted to pull him aside and warn him that he was trying too hard. He'd left moments ago to get a fresh drink for Dr. Hal Goff, leaving Mia alone with the mustached man in the plaid suit. Dr. Goff had barely spared her two words since Daniel introduced her as his date, but he'd leered at her throughout the conversation, making her wish she'd worn a turtleneck, cargo pants and boots rather than the beaded navy cocktail dress.

Now Dr. Goff leaned against the balcony railing, assessing her. "So, you're a small-business owner?" At her nod, he grinned, the bushy mustache twitching. "Are you by any chance a decorator? Because you would certainly brighten up any room you're in."

For Daniel's sake, rather than roll her eyes, she managed a small, artificial smile and tried not to psychically will Dr. Goff to tumble into the waiting pond below. "I'm an event planner." *Who should be working right now.*

She'd fought the urge at least ten times to text Shannon for updates on how the party was going. *Shannon knows what she's doing. She can handle the job.* It wasn't lack of faith in her employee that had Mia antsy; it was the unprecedented oddity of putting a man before her company. She'd never done that before. Daniel had been introducing her all night as simply "my date." But her willingness to suffer through this tonight proved that, for her, he was far more than someone she was casually dating.

What was she to him? After the reception tonight, they needed to talk.

Daniel returned with their refills, and she gratefully took her Sauvignon Blanc; if she ever had to come to another one of these, she was bringing a flask of hard liquor.

Goff sipped his beer, telling Daniel, "I've always thought highly of you—"

Difficult to believe since he'd greeted Daniel as "David" and had to be reminded twice what he taught.

"—but you must be even smarter than I realized to win over such a sexy creature."

"She is too good for me," Daniel agreed, meeting her eyes and promising without words that he would make this up to her.

If it was just people being pompous and obsequious, she could handle it, but Goff was being downright gross, his gaze locked on her breasts while Daniel tried to talk to him about some accreditation policy. Mia's temper rose. She wanted to snap, "My eyes are up here, jackass." But that seemed potentially damaging to Daniel's career.

Did her date even realize she was being mentally undressed? Or was he too focused on trying to make a good impression? Deciding that she couldn't count on him for tactful rescue, she decided to save herself.

Tapping Daniel on the shoulder—perhaps harder than strictly necessary—she interrupted him midsentence. "If you men will excuse me, I see Eli Wallace and I'd love to go say hi. Daniel, catch up with me later?"

Goff gave her another one of those oily smiles. "We hate for you to go, but we sure don't mind watching you walk away."

At that, Daniel blinked, his expression darkening. She'd appreciate the annoyance on her behalf more if it hadn't taken him so long to get a clue.

Rather than verbally shiv Dr. Goff, she spun on her heel and went into the living room. Luckily, Eli's height made him easy to spot even in a crowd. She'd been disappointed to learn that Bex couldn't make it tonight because she had rounds, but it was a relief to see Eli's friendly face.

He'd been chatting with two men but seemed happy to scoot aside and include her in their circle. "Mia, let me introduce Dr. Jay Patel, one of our guest professors this semester."

The man who shook her hand was one of those people who made glasses look hot.

"And Dr. Kevin Lerner," Eli added. "From our board of regents."

She shook his hand, too, mentally crossing her fingers that the man wasn't a blowhard like Goff. Luckily, Dr. Lerner was articulate, interesting and not drawn to her boobs as if by their gravitational pull. Chatting with him and supporting Eli's loyal praise of Daniel was no challenge at all.

Eventually, the provost interrupted to "borrow Dr. Lerner" and Dr. Patel asked to be pointed in the direction of the restroom.

Mia stood alone with Eli. "I'd hoped Daniel would have broken free of Goff by now." She watched the man in plaid gesture expansively while Daniel nodded several times but couldn't seem to get a word in edgewise. "Dude sure loves the sound of his own voice, doesn't he?"

Eli tried to smother a chuckle. "Yes, but that dude also oversees major university decisions, so…"

"So I should show more tact?" She hadn't shoved him off the balcony; that was pretty tactful of her.

Keeping her voice to a whisper, she asked, "Tell me the truth—is Bex really at the hospital tonight, or was that just an excuse so she could stay home in yoga pants and watch Netflix? Because, if that's the case, I'm leaving to join her."

Eli laughed. "Not all of these gatherings are so awful. People are tense right now because so many important things will be voted on at next week's meeting and everyone's hoping to sway the decisions. You'll see, next time you come to one of these—"

"Oh, hell no." She shuddered. "Netflix and yoga pants, remember?" When they'd first arrived, Daniel had mentioned that three members of the board of regents were here. "He's had plenty of face time with Goff, and you and I talked him up to Dr. Lerner—who, frankly, seemed smart enough to vote in Daniel's favor anyway. Who's the other regent?" She was feeling very goal oriented; maybe if she engaged whoever it was in conversation, Daniel could join them, do a few minutes of networking, then get her out of there.

"Dr. Carolyn Hollis." Eli discreetly gestured to a blonde woman holding court in the corner of the room. She was wearing the same sparkly sweater set Mia's stepmother had on at dinner.

"I'll go see if I can wiggle into her entourage," Mia said wearily. "Will you let Daniel know where I am? If Goff hasn't decided to vote for him by now, he ain't gonna."

As Mia approached the throng surrounding Carolyn, she realized the woman was passionately discussing politics; maybe Daniel mentioning that his brother was in politics would give him a conversational opening. Five minutes later, however, Mia had revised her opinion. Carolyn Hollis didn't enjoy talking politics. What she enjoyed was snidely explaining to every person around her why their political beliefs were wrong. The crowd around her thinned as Carolyn implied that anyone who didn't agree with her was too stupid to be working for the university in the first place. She swiveled her sharklike gaze to Mia as if sensing fresh blood.

"And what do you teach? Or, are you an administrator?" Carolyn demanded.

Nice try, but I don't work for the college, so I don't have to kiss your ass. "Neither. My date is a lit professor here, but I'm an event planner. I coordinate galas and charity events and weddings."

"Oh, I just love weddings." Carolyn's expression softened unexpectedly. "My daughter's getting married in the spring. Do you have a card? She has a coordinator, of course, but you never know when you'll have to fire someone." With that zealous gleam in her eye, she seemed almost hopeful.

"You know, I carry them in my regular purse but forgot to bring them tonight," Mia lied, holding up the tiny evening bag that matched her dress. She didn't particularly want to work with this woman—or poach clients from whatever poor coordinator was having to currently deal with her—but at least weddings gave them a safe topic until Daniel got his butt over there.

They discussed music selections and receptions and Mia ended up pulling out her phone to show Carolyn pictures. "This is actually from the first wedding I handled," Mia said, smiling in fond recollection. "James and Steve wanted—"

"Two men?" Carolyn eyed her with disdain. "So you do novelty weddings, not real ones?"

Mia recoiled. "Exactly what about two people in love pledging their lives to one another isn't 'real' enough for you?"

Carolyn's eyes narrowed, color climbing in her cheeks. "Now, see here—"

"There you are." Daniel slid his arm around Mia's shoulders, his expression tense. "Did you still want to leave?" To Carolyn, he said, "She had a headache earlier and was indulging me by staying a few more minutes. We should go."

Even though she wanted to leave, Mia resented his polite lie. It seemed as if she was being dragged away like a child who'd misbehaved.

Carolyn drew herself up, glaring. "It's too bad you aren't feeling well," she told Mia, "but that's really no excuse for rudeness."

"*I* was rude? Manners were the only thing that kept me from—"

"*Mia.*" A muscle in Daniel's jaw twitched. "We're leaving. I'm sorry we didn't go earlier."

Yeah? Well she was sorry she'd come with him in the first place.

Mia supposed it was no great surprise that Daniel barely spoke to her on the ride back to her apartment. He was in classic Keegan shutdown mode, stone-faced and radiating disapproval. She could break the silence, but she was waging an internal battle, torn between apologizing and defending her actions. It was dinner with his parents all over again.

Thinking about his family reminded her of their fondness for Felicity. Mia would bet money that his ex-girlfriend would never have lashed out at a regent, no matter how provoked.

"I don't belong in your world," she said as Daniel parked the car.

His head jerked sharply toward her. He opened his mouth as if he might argue, but then didn't.

Because he knows I'm right. "We're very different people. We've known that since college."

He couldn't argue with that, either.

Was he going to say anything at all? *Maybe it's better if he doesn't.* Getting the words out was hard enough without interruption or disagreement. "On our very first date, you told me you thought of me as abrasive. I'm not sure why we didn't just cut our losses then. I'm never going to be like Felicity or Rachel, who's good-natured enough to ignore your parents when they belittle her. That's not me." And if he tried to shame her into becoming someone else, she'd hate him for it.

"No one asked you to be Felicity or Rachel," he grated.

Maybe not outright. "You didn't like how I handled dinner with your family. You didn't like how I handled tonight. And you have a right to be upset. You'll still have to deal with your relatives and colleagues long after we stop sleeping together. I get that my words and actions affect you. But I don't want to date a guy who can't support my words and actions, who wants me to be…less me." She wanted to be with a man who, if he couldn't bring himself to stand up for her, at least didn't object when she stood up for herself.

Eli had mentioned her attending more faculty mixers in the future. That would be part of a relationship with Daniel, a real relationship. An affair was easy because it was just the sex, but when you were truly *with* a person, you had to deal with their job and their family and their baggage, too. She didn't want that. And based on his proposing to a woman who was pretty much Mia's polar opposite, Mia wasn't what he wanted, either. Not really, not long term.

She reached blindly for the door handle, tears blurring her vision. "The last few weeks have been—"

"You're really walking away? Over Carolyn Hollis being insufferable?"

"If you think that's why I'm walking away, you haven't been paying attention," she said sadly. "I have solid reasons."

"That can be overcome," he insisted, "if you aren't too stubborn to compromise!"

"You mean change?"

He glanced away, his expression guilty. She suspected it was the closest he would come to admitting he needed her to be different to fit comfortably into his life.

"Goodbye, Daniel."

He didn't chase after her or offer to make any compromises of his own. Mia wasn't surprised. She was just hollow and heartbroken.

"Two down and one to go," Mrs. Kendrick said with a fond glance at Wren. "It's nice to see my girls with men who make them happy. I'm just sorry your young man couldn't make it tonight, dear, we were looking forward to meeting him."

Wren smiled at her mother over the rim of her champagne flute; Mia couldn't help noticing the expression didn't quite reach her eyes. "Brant's sorry, too. But, family emergency—no getting around that."

When Mrs. Kendrick headed toward the entrance to greet newly arrived guests, Mia sidled closer to her friend. "Is there really a family emergency?"

"Could be. No idea. I haven't spoken to Brant in days, not since I broke up with him."

"You what?" Mia felt awful that she'd vented to her friend about ending the affair with Daniel and hadn't even noticed that Wren had her own problems. "I can't believe you didn't tell me."

"I didn't want the news getting out before Riley's engagement party. I don't want my family fussing over me when this should be her big night." She glanced around, lowering her voice. "But since you know now, it would be a relief to finally whine to someone. He and I were so much alike. It was maddening."

"At the beginning, you liked how much the two of you have in common." Of course, at the beginning of her affair with Daniel, it had all been giddy heat and mutual pleasure. Things changed.

"Turns out, that gets old fast. It's like if you were with someone and every time you tried to tell them a joke, they already knew the punch line. And you know how I'm super disorganized and flighty?"

"No comment."

"I have these cool ideas, like that Halloween party for charity you helped me plan, or the community garden I started at my apartment building, but I'm bad with details. So was Brant. If he and I ever lived together, we'd sit around sharing our grand ideas in the dark because neither of us had remembered to pay the electric bill. I started to have doubts after lunch with you and Riley, when we talked about how my future niece or nephew needs both aunts to balance each other out. There was no balance with me and Brant."

Mia bit her lip. "I don't know what the right answer is, but it's not so easy to date someone who's your opposite, either." She believed she'd done the right thing walking away from Daniel. But she'd missed him every single night since.

Wren squeezed her arm sympathetically. "I'm actually more upset about you and Daniel's breakup than I am about my own. You two were a good balance for each other."

Balance implied equal distribution. "I don't know. There was me on one side of the teeter-totter, up in the air and noticing how far away the ground looked, and the other side was bogged down with him and all the important university people I'd probably have to suck up to and his family, who would wage an unending campaign to change me. Hell, even *my* family. You should have seen the joy in their eyes when they thought I'd found a man who would be a 'good influence.'"

"Well, they're parents." Wren raised one shoulder in a half shrug. "They want you to be happy, and I'm sure they'd prefer you find that happiness with a smart, employed, solid citizen rather than a bank robber who's got you driving the getaway car."

That almost made Mia laugh.

Wren changed the subject. "Now that I'm single and not having sex regularly, I have a lot of extra time, so I've gone back to jewelry making." She set her huge purse on the high-top table between them; the bag hardly matched her dress, but she never went anywhere without it. In case of emergency, Wren could probably pull a tent and a generator out of there. "Here." She handed Mia a small velvet drawstring bag.

Inside was a gorgeous hand-beaded necklace. While Mia was oohing and aahing over it, Wren handed her two more bags. They contained a matching bracelet and a couple pairs of earrings.

"Just be glad I stopped before I got to a tiara," Wren said wryly. "I *really* miss the sex."

"I know what you mean." But if Mia were being honest with herself, she didn't just miss the sex. She missed him. His wry sense of humor had brightened her day so many times over the past month. And he'd been a great listener, especially the night they'd had dinner with her parents. And...

Dammit, listing all of the things that made him wonderful was not going to help her miss him less. It only made her throat burn and her eyes prick with tears.

"Will you excuse me?" she asked her friend. "I want to find the ladies' room, then check to make sure Riley and Jack don't need anything."

She darted through the crowd, hoping no one saw her cry. But, since this was an engagement party, if necessary, she could say she was choked up for the happy couple.

Yeah, tears of joy. Not at all tears of disappointment and regret that she'd fallen in love with the wrong man. And lost him.

DANIEL HAD DRAGGED himself to the black-tie fundraiser because he'd promised his family he'd attend—and because it beat moping at home over Mia. But given the way he'd been snarling at people left and right, his parents were probably now wishing that he'd canceled. Only moments ago, he'd snapped at his mother for making critical comments about Rachel's dress.

"I think she looks lovely," he defended his sister-in-law, "and I certainly didn't hear her ask for your opinion."

His mother drew back as if he'd slapped her, cheeks mottled, but across the table, Rachel beamed at him. For all that Rachel never complained, why should she have to put up with nitpicky remarks or condescension? *I should have said something to my parents years ago.*

Actually, no. His brother should have said something in his wife's defense, as a show of support that they were a united front. If he'd supported Mia at the faculty reception—told leering Dr. Goff to take his damn eyeballs out of her cleavage and put them back in his head or even silently allowed Mia to conclude her own conversation with Carolyn Hollis—maybe Mia would be with him now. In which case, she would have plenty to say about this fund-raiser. There'd been no vegetarian entrée option at the high-dollar buffet, and the band's music was putting people to sleep rather than engaging them.

His mother touched the edge of his sleeve, her expression conciliatory. "I'm going to overlook how rude you were—"

The way Rachel had overlooked Mrs. Keegan's rudeness for years?

"—because I know you're probably just cranky after breaking up with that woman. But I assure you, it's for the best. She wasn't right for you."

"Mother, if you say Felicity's name, I'm leaving." It wasn't an idle threat, he realized. He was prepared to get up and exit the ballroom right now, to hell with her ire. He respected his parents, but he couldn't live his life to please them. "In fact, if you try to push her back into my life, this will be the last fund-raiser I attend all year."

"Don't be ridiculous. Your brother is running for governor."

"And I wish him luck. He should go to lots of fund-raisers, shake a lot of hands. But it's his campaign not mine. I've never wanted the spotlight, and I don't want Felicity Green." He wanted Mia. He knew it with a clarity so sharp that it pierced through him; he wouldn't

have been surprised to see actual blood on his tux-
edo shirt.

Which begged the question—if he wanted her so
badly, why was he here at a boring fund-raiser he
hadn't wanted to attend in the first place instead of
fighting for her?

He almost bolted from his seat then and there. His
mother studied him, her expression alarmed.

"Are you all right?" she asked.

No. He was miserable without Mia. With each day
that passed, he second-guessed his actions and words,
wishing he'd handled things differently. She'd given
him a second chance. If he figured out how to apologize, was there any possibility she'd give him a third?
"You're wrong when you say Mia isn't right for me."
He only hoped *he* was right for *her*.

Mrs. Keegan paled. "You really care about her so
much?"

"I do. I know that's not what you want to hear, but
you have to give up this insane dream of controlling
who I love."

"Daniel! My intentions were to be helpful, not controlling. Felicity's a wonderful girl, and your father and
I truly thought she would make you happy. That's what
we want for our children—happiness."

"And the governor's mansion," he said wryly.

"Well, yes, that, too. But winning that election
would make your brother happy. Just like getting tenure makes you happy."

Not as much as he would have expected. The news
had come yesterday, and Eli had taken him out to cel-

ebrate. Daniel had tried to be appropriately jovial, but not being able to share his success with Mia had dulled the victory. "Mia makes me happy."

His mother sighed. "Then I'm sure your father and I will learn to love her. In time."

He smiled, touched despite his bleak mood. "Thanks, Mom." Did that mean Mia could learn to eventually love them?

More important, was there any chance she could ever love *him*?

WHEN MIA CAME back from lunch on Monday, the office door was locked. Shannon hadn't mentioned that she would be out that afternoon, but maybe she'd had errands to run. Or maybe she'd gone upstairs to visit Paige. Apparently, their date over the weekend had been a big success.

I told you, Shannon had grinned this morning, *that I'd make my move when I was ready.*

Mia was glad someone's love life was working out. She dug through her purse for the keys she hadn't expected to need. Then she opened the door, making a mental list of—

Her heart stopped. "Daniel."

He was sitting on a picnic blanket in the middle of her reception area, a bottle of champagne chilling in an ice bucket next to him.

"What the hell are you doing here?" she asked.

"Waiting for you," he said simply.

She narrowed her eyes, sensing conspiracy. "You sent Shannon away."

"More like she enthusiastically volunteered."

So much for not interfering in each other's personal lives. Mia had some choice words for her friend when she came back.

Daniel stood and came toward her.

The closer he got, the faster her treacherous heart beat. *Stay strong.* "Daniel, this isn't like when you sent flowers. We didn't have a fight that you need to apologize for. We just aren't—"

"I love you."

Her vision swam, and she leaned against the door for support. "Wh-what?"

He tilted her chin up so that she was meeting his eyes, and the rush of pleasure she got just from that contact was so strong she almost nuzzled his hand. "I love you," he repeated.

"But that's a terrible idea!"

He chuckled darkly. "It wasn't exactly something I set out to do. I know you think we're too different to make this work, but I'm a lit professor. Going back centuries, you know what the great love stories have in common? It was never easy."

She swallowed back a tide of emotion. "This isn't Shakespeare, Daniel. It's my life." *My heart.*

"Mine, too. And my life feels flat and purposeless without you. I found out Friday that I got tenure—"

"Congratulations!"

"—and once I realized I couldn't celebrate it with you, I barely even cared. That's why I brought the champagne. I was hoping you'd celebrate with me now, that you'd give me another chance." He ran a thumb along her bottom lip, and she trembled. "I want to kiss you so damn badly."

Bad idea. If he did, she'd be lost. She ducked her head. "Daniel, I—" *love you, too* "—care about you a lot. But I don't think I'm what you need long term."

"You're wrong."

He said it with such confidence that she wanted to shriek in exasperation. It had been a lot easier to break up with him when he'd calmly gone along with it. It was more difficult to send away this man with the sexy gaze and declarations of love.

She switched tactics. "All right, maybe you aren't what I need—"

"I told my mother to be nicer to her daughters-in-law and to quit trying to control my love life and that *you're* the woman I want."

"You did?" That couldn't have gone over well.

"She's making her peace with it. My parents aren't terrible people, but I let them bully me for too long. No more." He smiled like a man with a weight lifted from his shoulders.

"I'm proud of you." Whatever happened between her and Daniel, she hoped he had a healthier relationship with his family going forward.

"I love my family," he said, "but I don't want to live my life for their approval. And I don't want to be the cold, judgmental bastard I was in college. I've worked to change that over the past decade, but a few weeks with you was more effective than any of my solo attempts. I don't want to revert to life as an ice cube."

He leaned in so close they were sharing breaths. "Keep melting me, Mia. Please."

She'd have to be made of solid ice to resist that voice. "I love you, too," she whispered.

His eyes widened with surprise and pleasure, and then he lifted her off the ground for a frenzied, open-mouthed kiss that was a celebration all its own. No champagne required. Heat flooded her veins as his tongue licked against hers, and she wrapped her legs around him, wanting to feel him everywhere at once. Wanting to tell him she loved him as he moved inside her.

Which would be a great plan if she didn't have a client meeting in twenty minutes. She bit his bottom lip. "You *had* to do this in the middle of a workday?"

"I couldn't wait until tonight. I already regret the lost hours we could've spent together."

"You're not an ice cube, you're a romantic."

"Not always," he cautioned. "We'll still argue. I know our perspectives are different—"

"I have it on good authority that being with someone who agrees with you on everything is boring as hell," she said, thinking of Wren.

Daniel laughed. "Honey, the one thing I can guarantee you is we'll never be boring."

This man was willing to make changes for her; she supposed she could make a few for him. Small ones—nothing that sacrificed who she was or what she believed in, but enough to show him that he was worth the effort. Worth her love. "Maybe we could try going out to dinner sometime with your parents," she said grudgingly. "Just the two of them, so they can focus on how great you are instead of your brother's potential future as the ruler of the free world." It couldn't be any more awkward than the twenty-minute conversation she'd had with Patience last night. The two of them might never be BFFs, but as Patience had gushed about how impressed she was that Mia built a company from scratch, some of Mia's old bitterness had faded.

Families were complicated, but she was willing to attempt making peace with the Keegans. "I don't know if I could ever be nice to Carolyn Hollis, though," she warned. "That woman was vile."

"I'm tenured now," he reminded her, "almost impossible to get rid of. You don't have to suck up to anyone on my behalf, I promise." The humor faded from his tone. "I'm sorry about that reception. I should have told Goff to go f—"

"I know how important your job is to you. I could have tempered my approach a little, too. But speaking of jobs, I'm afraid I have a meet—"

"Shannon cleared your afternoon," he told her, kissing the curve of her neck. Pleasure danced over her nerve endings.

"The whole afternoon?" Shannon was forgiven for her meddling. In fact, Mia was thinking about giving her friend a huge raise. "So how am I supposed to spend my time now?"

He nipped at her earlobe. "What does your shoulder devil suggest?"

"Oh, she has some ideas." Joy blossomed through

her, every bit as potent as the rising desire, and she tugged him down onto the picnic blanket, her fingers already freeing the buttons of his shirt. "Lots and *lots* of ideas…"

* * * * *

REQUEST YOUR FREE BOOKS!
2 FREE NOVELS PLUS 2 FREE GIFTS!

H HARLEQUIN®

Blaze

red-hot reads!

YES! Please send me 2 FREE Harlequin® Blaze® novels and my 2 FREE gifts (gifts are worth about $10). After receiving them, if I don't wish to receive any more books, I can return the shipping statement marked "cancel." If I don't cancel, I will receive 4 brand-new novels every month and be billed just $4.74 per book in the U.S. or $5.21 per book in Canada. That's a savings of at least 14% off the cover price. It's quite a bargain. Shipping and handling is just 50¢ per book in the U.S. and 75¢ per book in Canada.* I understand that accepting the 2 free books and gifts places me under no obligation to buy anything. I can always return a shipment and cancel at any time. Even if I never buy another book, the two free books and gifts are mine to keep forever.

150/350 HDN GH2D

Name _____ (PLEASE PRINT)

Address _____ Apt. #

City _____ State/Prov. _____ Zip/Postal Code

Signature (if under 18, a parent or guardian must sign)

Mail to the **Reader Service:**
IN U.S.A.: P.O. Box 1867, Buffalo, NY 14240-1867
IN CANADA: P.O. Box 609, Fort Erie, Ontario L2A 5X3

Want to try two free books from another line?
Call 1-800-873-8635 or visit www.ReaderService.com.

* Terms and prices subject to change without notice. Prices do not include applicable taxes. Sales tax applicable in N.Y. Canadian residents will be charged applicable taxes. Offer not valid in Quebec. This offer is limited to one order per household. Not valid for current subscribers to Harlequin Blaze books. All orders subject to credit approval. Credit or debit balances in a customer's account(s) may be offset by any other outstanding balance owed by or to the customer. Please allow 4 to 6 weeks for delivery. Offer available while quantities last.

Your Privacy—The Reader Service is committed to protecting your privacy. Our Privacy Policy is available online at www.ReaderService.com or upon request from the Reader Service.

We make a portion of our mailing list available to reputable third parties that offer products we believe may interest you. If you prefer that we not exchange your name with third parties, or if you wish to clarify or modify your communication preferences, please visit us at www.ReaderService.com/consumerschoice or write to us at Reader Service Preference Service, P.O. Box 9062, Buffalo, NY 14240-9062. Include your complete name and address.

HB15

SPECIAL EXCERPT FROM

HARLEQUIN Blaze

Regan Macintosh doesn't trust Jamie Quinn's roguish charm, but her resolve to keep the sexy stranger away is starting to wane…and if she's not careful, their hungry passion could make them both lose control.

Read on for a sneak preview of
THE MIGHTY QUINNS: JAMIE,
the latest book in Kate Hoffmann's beloved series
THE MIGHTY QUINNS.

Regan walked out into the chilly night air. A shiver skittered down her spine, but she wasn't sure it was because of the cold or due to being in such close proximity to Jamie. Her footsteps echoed softly on the wood deck, and when she reached the railing, Regan spread her hands out on the rough wood and sighed.

She heard the door open behind her and she held her breath, counting his steps as he approached. She shivered again, but this time her teeth chattered.

A moment later she felt the warmth of his jacket surrounding her. He'd pulled his jacket open and he stood behind her, his arms wrapped around her chest, her back pressed against his warm body.

"Better?"

It was better. But it was also more frightening. And more exhilarating. And more confusing. And yet it seemed perfectly natural. "I should probably get to bed," Regan said. "I can't afford to fall asleep at work tomorrow."

He slowly turned her around in his arms until she faced him. His lips were dangerously close to hers, so close she could feel the warmth of his breath on her cheek.

"I know you still don't trust me, but you're attracted to me. I'm attracted to you, too. I want to kiss you," he whispered. "Why don't we just see where this goes?"

"I think that might be a mistake," she replied.

"Then I guess we'll leave it for another time," he said. "Good night, Regan." With that he turned and walked off the deck.

Her heart slammed in her chest and she realized how close she'd come to surrender. He was right; she was attracted to him. She had wanted to kiss him. She'd been thinking about it all night. But in the end common sense won out.

Regan slowly smiled. She was strong enough. She *could* control her emotions when he touched her. Though he still was dangerous, he was just an ordinary guy. And if she could call the shots, maybe she could let something happen between them.

Maybe he'd ask to kiss her again tomorrow. Maybe then she'd say yes.

Don't miss
THE MIGHTY QUINNS: JAMIE
by Kate Hoffmann, available in February 2017
wherever Harlequin® Blaze® books and ebooks are sold.

www.Harlequin.com

HBEXP0117

Turn your love of reading into rewards you'll love with
Harlequin My Rewards

**Join for FREE today at
www.HarlequinMyRewards.com**

Earn **FREE BOOKS** of your choice.

Experience **EXCLUSIVE OFFERS** and contests.

Enjoy **BOOK RECOMMENDATIONS**
selected just for you.

PLUS! Sign up now
and get **500** points
right away!

Earn
FREE
REWARDS
Join
Today!
HarlequinMyRewards.com

MYR16R

Love the Harlequin book you just read?

Your opinion matters.

Review this book on your favorite book site, review site, blog or your own social media properties and share your opinion with other readers!

Be sure to connect with us at:
Harlequin.com/Newsletters
Facebook.com/HarlequinBooks
Twitter.com/HarlequinBooks

HARLEQUIN®

A *Romance* FOR EVERY MOOD™

JUST CAN'T GET ENOUGH?

Join our social communities
and talk to us online.

You will have access to the latest
news on upcoming titles and special
promotions, but most importantly,
you can talk to other fans about your
favorite Harlequin reads.

Harlequin.com/Community

 Facebook.com/HarlequinBooks

 Twitter.com/HarlequinBooks

Pinterest.com/HarlequinBooks

HARLEQUIN®

A *Romance* FOR EVERY MOOD™

Stay up-to-date on all your romance-reading news with the *Harlequin Shopping Guide*, featuring bestselling authors, exciting new miniseries, books to watch and more!

The newest issue will be delivered right to you with our compliments! There are 4 each year.

Signing up is easy.

EMAIL

ShoppingGuide@Harlequin.ca

WRITE TO US

HARLEQUIN BOOKS
Attention: Customer Service Department
P.O. Box 9057, Buffalo, NY 14269-9057

OR PHONE

1-800-873-8635 in the United States
1-888-343-9777 in Canada

Please allow 4-6 weeks for delivery of the first issue by mail.